Brother Kell's Book of Spells:

Cormac Returns for a Spell

Book II

by Michael F. Brain

Published by Pen It! Publications, LLC
812-371-4128 www.penitpublications.com

ISBN: 978-1-954004-84-9
Edited by Wanda Williams
Cover Design by Donna Cook

Character List

Esquire Cormac O'Briain aka Gunnarson
Lady Moya O'Briain aka Gunnarson
Sir Skeggi Gunnarson
Julia Gunnarson, a baby
Rognvald-step brother to Skeggi
Earl Thorkel of Orkney*
Captain Huw ap Preselli
Earl Edwin of Eccleston manor, a widower
Lady Grainne, his daughter
Tudno, a hermit priest *
Brother Galen
Rollo de Bretton
The Reeve of Chester
Brocmale, Earl of Chester *
Lady Hilda, wife of Brocmale
Peter, Bishop of Chester and Lichfield*
Vern O'The Mill
Peter Akimbo
Ron Rose

*Characters in history

Dedication

This book is dedicated to my wife, Jean Brain.

FAMILY HOME

It had now been 4 years since the Gunnarson family had settled on the River Dee near Chester, and it had seemed like an eternity for the betrothed Lady Grainne and Esquire Cormac. Prolonged absences had been necessitated by studies that had kept them apart, except for all too short reunions at Holy festivals of Easter and Yuletide. Earl Edwin had watched with delighted pride and satisfaction that his only daughter had blossomed into a confident and beautiful young woman of 15 years. As for Sir Skeggi Gunnarson (once a Viking) and his wife Lady Moya, they now had a baby daughter they named Julia, and like her older brother she had inherited her father's fiery red hair.

Although some Norse words were used in private, now they were quite fluent speaking the Saxon tongue. Their new home was named Portmore Manor and it had been a year since the local architect and builders, on loan from the Abbey, had completely renovated the ancient remains of the Roman villa being able to use some of the original stone. Astonished, when many weeds had been cleared away, a mosaic floor had been revealed. In a weedy pond they had also discovered a marble statue of Minerva. New vines had been planted and the orchards were bearing delicious fruit, in season. A wine press and barrel storage had yet to be started, also the fermentation vats, but the local Monks were regularly consulted.

Cormac's return home and his long-anticipated graduation from Wroxeter Abbey School was now tinged with sadness, as Grandfather Bedwyr O' Briain had died peacefully in his sleep, only a few month's short of his 60th birthday. At his funeral Abbott Peter led the service of thanksgiving, celebrating his life, and his daughter Moya wept and cried out," Not even three score years and ten mentioned in the Bible."

Bedwyr had doted upon his young grandson during his childhood years and Cormac had listened enthralled to grandfather's tales of the Celtic saints, the brave chieftains of Ireland, and most of all being told that their ancestor was Brother Kell. Yet more changes awaited Cormac, as his uncle Rognvald (his father's stepbrother) had decided to return to Orkney and serve the Viking Earl Thorkel, taking his share of the Pirate Hoard, feeling too restless to share the quiet life as an honoured guest at Portmore Manor.

Trader Captain Huw ap Preselli was a welcome guest at Portmore Manor when his ship docked in Chester and would entertain the families of Earl Edwin and Sir Skeggi with tales of his voyages. They would reminisce of the adventures he had shared with Moya and Cormac when they had left Ireland and raise a toast to old Bedwyr. Earl Edwin would remind them of the exploits of Cormac, Grainne and Rognvald that had led to him being rescued from the Liuerpul Slaver Pirates, some four years ago.

Graduated

Portmore Manor now had a watchtower next to its River Dee landing stage entrance, together with a guard and a horn to alert Sir Skeggi and Lady Moya of the arrival of guests and warns them of intruders. Cormac and his horse arrived from Chester by a new flat-bottomed ferry boat. He smiled, glad to be home now that his studies were finished, but the horse, Kelly, was startled by the loud noise of the horn. He held the reins tightly in his well-muscled arms, or his steed might have jumped into the water.

Last time he was home, he had been pleased to see that the moat had been stocked with edible fishes.

Now he led Kelly down the path to his home, and saw his parents coming to meet him, with a wet nurse carrying baby Julia. The manor had seen many changes and improvements, and the latest was a moat that was fed by a channel from the river and delivered by a sluice gate. A little distance behind them was his beloved Grainne who was wearing a very becoming gown, and he notice with youthful appreciation, the firm swell of her bosom, her cherry red lips and pretty ribbons in her hair. Even from a distance she had noticed his red hair, longer now and covered with a jaunty hat, but much more than that, he had now grown so tall and passed the height of his father. His face was lightly tanned by regular exposure to the sun, and he carried a scroll of vellum tied with a red ribbon, and a short dagger in his belt.

His parents now opened their arms to greet him with a big hug, and he thought, *I am a little too old for this now, and I am impatient to be alone with Grainne.* He then bent down to lift his baby sister from the arms of Nurse Mary, kissing her head and tickled her under the chin, to her evident delight. It was now the turn of his betrothed and they held hands and looked at each other, wordlessly, feeling so full of emotion now that their time apart was ended. To all of them he said proudly, "Here is my scroll that says I graduated summa cum laude, which means with the highest honours and I ended my final year as Head Boy; thanks to Brother Kell I excelled in Latin and Greek. They want me to study Law, but maybe later, for now, I want to expand our family business by shipping and trade." His parents were overjoyed and so proud, but colouring a little, Grainne realised how confident, handsome, and muscular he had grown, and with a delicious tremor that suffused her body, she realised, so desirable.

Now the family group made their way to the manor crossing the drawbridge, into the courtyard with its tinkling fountain, and on into the entrance flanked by the servants who bowed low to the young master- "No ceremony" he said, "it's just me, Cormac home at last. It is so good to see you all, and I have brought you all small gifts back from Wroxeter, cheeses and mead that the monks excel in making." Turning to Grainne he whispered, "I have a special gift for you."

Ancestors

Later that happy day, they were joined by Earl Edwin who was returning from another round of talks with his rich friends and Aldermen concerning the proposed 'New Deva Trading Company', hoping to finally persuade them to back this new venture by buying shares to fund it. So far Edwin and Skeggi with Bishop Peter had been the most vigorous in promoting the scheme, but over-cautious small business owners were reluctant, especially when it involved buying a ship and fitting it out to sail the Middle Sea.

Taking Cormac's hand, she led him down the path to the landing stage to greet her father. Now a recent graduate in Natural Philosophy, and full of confidence in the company of important men, Esquire Cormac shook the hand of the man he had rescued those four years ago. He was expecting him to say condescendingly, "My how you have grown, young man," but to his enormous gratitude and pride he merely said, "The Abbott has already informed me that you have completed your education magnificently, and my delight is that you have returned to my daughter, ready to be much more than just her betrothed. '

"My Lord Earl," he replied "Your sponsorship made my entry into Wroxeter Abbey School and went a good way to me being accepted. I understand you were a pupil there once?" Then it was time for Grainne to embrace her father in the demure and dignified manner expected of a well-schooled rich young heiress, but feeling so happy, she just grinned and kissed his forehead, saying "We welcome you. Do please join the Gunnarson family back at the manor, -we have wine waiting in their garden bower and the small, sweet cakes you like. I baked them myself, having had lessons from Lady Moya."

After more friendly greetings, the steward brought the wine and the cakes on a silver platter, and Cormac stood and proposed a Toast "To our families, may we soon enjoy the blessings of closer ties and to prosperity and honourable dealings in our joint venture. Now that we are almost family Lord Edwin, if my father agrees, I would like to know more about his own ancestry and why I was christened Cormac."

At this, his mother Moya pulled a wry face, and said, "Must we? Do we have to hear exaggerated tales of your Viking forefathers?"

"'But dear Mother," he replied, "this final year, my group of closest friends were always pestering me for just such an account. Most of their fathers were Saxon landowners and warrior chiefs who have never sailed any of the seven seas."

Sir Skeggi laughed uproariously saying, "Even I have only sailed one sea around these coasts that the Romans named Albion."

REVELATION AND EXPLANATION

The two families joined in the laughter and Skeggi spoke again, "My father, Magnus, son of Thorfinn the Bloodless, came from Iceland and when drunk would regale us with long tales about Njarl, but he never sailed away going a-Viking for plunder. He loved maps and old records of voyages, and that's what began my interest in learning to be a navigator. As to your name, priests of the White Christ had come to teach us a new way to live. We heard stories of a famous missionary Christian navigator called Columba, who had a friend he called Cormac-of-the-Sea. That Cormac, who was attacked by sea monsters in the seas around Orkney and the Shetlands, later was made Bishop of Durrow. I wanted you to have that name too. But you my dear brave Cormac are famous among our families for ridding us of monsters in human form-those Pirate Slavers!"

Then Grainne joined the conversation," He was blessed with more than a little help from Brother Kell's Book of Holy cards, and how did my Cormac always seem to know where you were, Sir Skeggi?"

Now Lady Moya put her finger to her lips and said, "For now that is a family secret. Those holy cards are now an heirloom and safely stored away from prying eyes, the hermit of Skellig entrusted them into my son's keeping, to be used only in times of great peril or need. They are what brought our two families together, and I thank God for that gift, every day."

Cormac now stood up and whispered to his father who nodded in agreement. Together they spoke gravely to their family and honoured guests and Cormac said in hushed tones, "Soon our families will be joined as one when the plans of my wedding to Grainne are approved and finalised, but now I urge you, on pain of death and eternal damnation not to speak to another living soul what father and I will reveal to you." After some gasps of surprise and delight Sir Skeggi said, "Please follow us to the new stables," so the group trooped out, with the ladies whispering and smiling.

First Cormac fetched a burning torch and a broom and opened the doors to where his horse Kelly whinnied a welcome, and Grainne stroked the horse's nose. He swept aside the straw and dung that covered the floor to reveal an iron ring set into a trapdoor; some steps were revealed that led down into a newly constructed underground chamber.

Entering first, his father led the way and lit another torch held in a wall sconce, handing the torch back to Cormac. Selecting a heavy key from a ring of other keys, his father opened the lock in a large iron-bound door, there was a second lock and Cormac solemnly produced another key hidden in the heel of his boot. Then the door swung open noiselessly to reveal several chests, stacked one upon another.

The Greater Treasure

Skeggi then ascended the steps and climbed through the trapdoor, leaving it held open by a hook and chain, to let in more light, and walked Cormac's horse outside, securing her halter to a ring set in the outer wall. Then he sat in front of the stable door with an axe on his lap, taking no chances with an intruder, however unlikely, or if a servant should come looking for them. Back in the hidden chamber, more torches were lit in other sconces, and Cormac began his explanatory performance.

The first chest was opened and seen to contain Navigation devices that a proud Viking had already shown and demonstrated to his son-displaying his sun shadow board, a sunstone, and the lodestone. Cormac had even written a short navigation scroll for the school library, based on his father's teachings, and another copy as lodged here.

The second chest contained some of the jewellery and precious metal plates and chalices that remained after using the others to pay for re-building Portmore Manor.

The third chest contained two Viking helmets, one old, dented and tarnished, the other dazzling, highly polished silver bronze and gold. Cormac held up the helmets in each hand. And asked, "Which do you think is the most prized by my father?" Earl Edwin naturally reached for the expensive looking one, and when he put it on and turned to show the ladies, Cormac swiftly donned the tarn helm, slipped behind the trio and they heard Cormac's voice echo around the chamber, "The wrong choice." All three were startled and called out in unison," Cormac where are you, are you hiding?" Chuckling mischievously, he moved to the open iron- bound door and took off the tarn helm, to reveal himself.

"What is this trickery?" exclaimed the Earl angrily, while the ladies stood open mouthed in wonder. Cormac began to explain the story of how his father had discovered a helmet fashioned by ancient dwarves for heroes favoured by the Norse Gods. First, he placed the tarn helm on the pretty head of his betrothed saying softly, "There is nothing to fear, it makes you invisible while you are wearing it."

Now the others were convinced when one by one they wore and then removed the helm, each time disappearing from the other's sight! Cormac retrieved the tarn helm and told the tale of how becoming invisible had helped his father escape serious injury in many battles, but more importantly, reveal and vanquish the assassin attempt on Chester's Bishop Peter and Earl Brocmale lives, four years ago.

Cormac could see that they were all wide-eyed with the wonder they had experienced, and continued, "Now we open the last chest," and revealed a highly decorated pack of cards, some with the image of Saints and others depicting farmyard animals, and still others of fantastic beasts. "Let us ascend from the chamber and the leave the stables for I have yet more wonders to reveal. First my father will come and assist me in locking the strong room door, and then we will disguise the trapdoor, and return my horse Kelly to his stable." They left the scene, glad to return to normality but careful not to be overheard by the servants.

Cormac drew Grainne to one side as the others walked thoughtfully and quietly back to the manor, and then he led her into the garden and sat her on the stone bench in an arbour. "No more delays and distractions, here is the special gift I promised you." Opening a small soft leather pouch, he took out a gold ring with a rare jewel and slipped it on her finger. She gasped in delight and threw her arms around him, kissed him tenderly and exclaimed, "Blue is my favourite colour, how did you come by this gem?" He answered, "A goldsmith visited my school in Wroxeter, having delivered a commission for the Abbott, our head tutor. I consulted him as to having him make me a gold ring, using as an example of size, one of your silver rings your father had given you last year, and he secretly loaned it to me. The craftsman took its measure, and then suggested he set a blue stone of polished moonstone cabochon in the ring. I told him to inscribe on the inside of the ring: *TE AMOR GRAINNE*." Then with a practised courtly bow, he got down on one knee and said, "I know we were formally betrothed, but now I ask you to marry me, my darling girl." She now joined him and also kneeling replied, "Ever since that day you rescued me adrift on the sea, my heart was yours, and now I gladly accept your proposal."

They both stood up and embraced passionately, and Grainne whispered, "These last two years while you have been away, I have had private instruction on the ways of marriage, both from your mother and Lady Hilda. We did spend some time giggling indiscreetly about the expectations of a husband..."

Cormac blushed and replied, "My tutors and some of my friends who had older married brothers gave some biological advice, while the monks muttered about *'birds and bees'*. "Like many young newlyweds, we will eventually find out what is pleasing for each other?" They both laughed joyously and ran into the manor with the glad news that their parents had been anticipating.

The two families were waiting expectantly in the main room, (before his return Cormac had written to Earl Edwin, formally asking permission to marry Grainne after he knew he had graduated), and they saw two joyful radiant faces approaching them. Earl Edwin and Sir Skeggi exclaimed, "Welcome to the family," in unison and the Lady Moya rushed over, held both their hands, and cried, "The dearest daughter I could wish for." The happy group retired for a celebration feast, and the laughter and the speeches brought smiles to the servants, except one, the groom that had been usurper Rollo's servant.

Both fathers and Cormac began to discuss plans for a new venture, should the proposed New Deva Trading Company not be agreed by the Chester Guilds. The ladies talked animatedly about new clothes, the wedding ceremony, and flowers, and speculated who would be Cormac's best man?

FETCH THE HELM

Meeting again after the heady bliss of yesterday when Grainne had joyfully agreed to be Cormac's wife, the two fathers now felt frustrated at the many delays some members of Chester's Council of Guilds had caused to Cormac's plans for a new trading Company. Some Town Council meetings had been in private and did not include Earl Edwin and Sir Skeggi, and it seemed a group of Guild members were wary of their monopolies being eroded and were further dismayed that Captain Huw ap Preselli may no longer favour them with special rates. "This impasse must end," Edwin said to his future son-in-law. While Cormac's father uttered a few Viking oaths that only his son only partly understood, that featured some anatomically impossible misadventures befalling some tardy Guilds members.

"Fetch me the tarn helm," thundered Skeggi, and Cormac raced off to covertly retrieve it, secretly glad his father had not asked for his war axe! "You must join us in the meeting this afternoon Cormac, but enter unseen wearing my tarn helm and overhear any dissenting mutterings."

"Gladly father," he replied, but felt disappointed as he had planned to go walking by the river with Grainne and would have to explain and apologise to her.

It was time to write up a document that explained the merits and large profits to be gained by being appointed Board Members of the proposed NEW DEVA TRADING COMPANY. The plan was that Groups of shares or single shares would be issued, only to members, for a fee that would then fund the venture. This was agreed, and so they sent for a lawyer and a notary to prepare the documents for signatures.

If some of Chester's wealthy Guilds and leaders could still not agree, then they still had some financial backing from local Bishops and Monasteries. They would explain to the meeting that Captain Huw would be a board member and his ship would be hired for the first voyage and from the profits, they would buy and refit another vessel. It would be of a plank design Carvel, with a triangular studding sail, top mast and top gallant sails he had recently seen in Brittany and provided a drawing on vellum.

The documents completed, the trio were the first to solemnly sign their names, and mounting their horses and saying farewells, they left for Chester by ferry. As they trotted through the town gates, guarded by men with swords and spears, they were admitted within the walls. Down the main street (once known as Via Principa), they came across a group of Vintners Guild members and greeted them by name, observing that they had already met elsewhere, probably in one of their taverns. Next, they saw the Guild of Tanners and Dyers, and trailing behind them the Guild of Goldsmiths and Moneylenders, and then the Guilds of Weavers and Carpenters. Cormac took a particular interest in the carpenters, who he would approach later about making a chariot.

New Venture

Before the trio entered the meeting, they agreed that Earl Edwin should be their spokesman who would then call upon recently graduated Cormac to answer questions. The Meeting Hall was almost full, and they noticed the various factions grouped together around the table. Then Edwin greeted the assembly, reminded them of the opportunities the proposed NEW DEVA TRADING COMPANY would bring, and asked if guilds would support this venture? "We will withdraw now while you consider the document I have prepared," said Edwin, and as they left the room many loud voices were heard arguing. Our trio left the room and waited to be asked to return, and Cormac donned the tarn helm and disappeared from sight, silently opening the door he closed it quickly and slowly walked around the table, listening to the conversations, some whispered furtively.

He heard some of the Moneylenders saying they were willing to buy shares as a guild, but also wanted to charge the rest of the groups and individuals if they provided a bond to cover the cost of possible shipwreck? This idea was well received, especially by the more cautious investors. So, Cormac left the room unobserved removed the helm and relayed the news. The door now reopened, and the trio were recalled to the investors meeting.

Once more Earl Edwin stood before them, and remarked, "I am sure you have more questions and need reassurances." Then he proudly introduced his future son-in-law Esquire Cormac Gunnarson, a recent graduate 'Summa Cum Laude' of Wroxeter Abbey School. "My alma mater," he chuckled.

Cormac stood tall and outwardly confident, after all he reminded himself, he did well in the debating classes. He began to address them in the Saxon tongue, saying, "Thank you one and all for allowing me to speak before such a wise and distinguished gathering of those who make this town prosperous. During my studies at the Abbey school, I made many friends who have influential fathers, and my tutors were delighted at my knowledge of the ancient Roman and Greek tongues. They allowed me access to their famous library where I discovered many dusty old books and scrolls that had hardly ever been opened.

"Those Greeks and Romans were renowned for their voyages and trading exploits that brought much wealth to their Leaders and citizens, and I found maps of islands in the Middle Sea where precious metals and gems were mined, places that grew fruits that are new to us. Using my father, Sir Skeggi's navigation skills, and my knowledge of languages, this new venture will bring great prosperity to those who join us by buying shares and becoming board members of this new Trading Company."

Cormac now felt a stir of interest, so he began to set forth a larger vision, not yet discussed with his family. "When our first trading mission has been successful, I have plans for establishing a trading post and warehouse and will need permission from the Ruler of the island of Kypros and its main port Pafos. You may know it as Cyprus where the blessed Saint Paul visited; it is at a crossroads for trade with lands to the East, sacred Palestine and fabled Constantinople, a place of great wealth."

Traders and Shipmates

The town meeting was a success, and many shares were pledged by signing the NEW DEVA TRADING COMPANY document, it would now be a time waiting while the money was raised by Guilds and individuals. Edwin already had pledges from local earls, and a trustworthy treasurer would need to be appointed, preferably an Abbott, used to dealing with gifts of money. Our trio would be nominated as Primary Owners, but further appointments as Company Officers would need to follow and allowances made for a future share issue. For our two families, it was time for a double celebration, and welcome back Captain Huw, recently returned from Brittany where he says they speak a form of the Welsh tongue.

Riding home our happy trio cautiously welcomed the support of the town council, but the fathers then exclaimed in unison to Cormac, "You might have given us forewarning of your grand scheme of a trading post and warehouse. Nevertheless, we are so proud of you, the money spent on your education will carry us through into the future. However, we will need more money to hire a ship and make Captain Huw a partner."

Cormac grinned happily, and replied, "Giving our investors a push to join us when untold riches beckon, while our family takes most of the risk, was what was needed. I need to speak to Brother Galen to persuade him to join our venture, as long sea voyages need a priest and a healer."

"Talking of a priest, who will be invited to perform the church wedding, Earl Edwin?" asked Cormac.

Edwin replied, "For my precious daughter and you my fine young man, nothing less than Abbot Peter!"

Then Sir Skeggi spoke, "Moya has told me that she would be most happy having a small wedding with only a few guests of your choice, and maybe a celebration afterwards for the servants and workers of both our houses, with music and dancing to remind us of the simple traditions left behind in Portmore."

They reached the manor of Portmore first, and Earl Edwin began to bid them farewell for the evening and ride on, but Cormac asked if he could go with him and spend some time with his bride to be. "My father will have much to tell my mother, and she will have many questions and her own opinions, no doubt," he said wryly. "But if you will think on the matter of a dowry, as I would not wish to offend tradition, but in all honesty, our family does not need money."

Turning to his father he said, with a sheepish smile "A special gift we would like from both of you, is to pay for a chariot to be made by a carpenter and a wheelwright to some plans I have brought home from Wroxeter. Then I can arrive at the church in style and drive my bride home!"

So, Edwin and Cormac rode on, while Skeggi was left to explain this unusual request to Moya.

FRUITFUL DISCUSSIONS

Earl Edwin and Cormac spoke quietly to each other as they rode back to Ecclestone Manor with the news THE NEW DEVA TRADING COMPANY now had shareholders and Grainne seeing them at the gates had a groom fetch her horse and then rode out to meet them. Before the men could dismount, Grainne asked," I know you both have news of our business success, but I would like to ride a while with my fiancée, please, oh and Captain Huw is waiting to see you." Her father agreed and said that he had much to discuss with his steward and the Captain.

The two young lovers rode on for a while and then stopped to let their horses drink from a stream, and then dismounted, Cormac gallantly getting off his steed first to help his beloved alight, though he knew she was a better rider than he. He held her in a gentle embrace, and they kissed tenderly and said, "I would like to hear what plans you and my mother have made for our wedding and the celebration that will follow, but first a question about apples." At that she laughed softly and ran her hand through his hair, and replied, "Apples, but you have orchards of them growing at Portmore Manor.

"No," he replied, "as a child did you ever play at Apple Bobbing?"

"Of course, all my friends, especially the girls played the game. Because our parents jokingly told us, if the apple we caught in our teeth was placed under our pillow, we would dream of the man we would marry."

Cormac grinned playfully and put his arms around her slender waist, and asked," Who did you dream of, then?"

She stood up, and holding both his hands she answered, "Oh it was some lad I used to pine for when we saw him in church on Sundays." She saw him immediately make a sad face, and quickly she continued, "Just teasing you Cormac, what I saw I dismissed, as it was a stranger with red hair, it is only just now you jogged my memory, and I see that even back then , you were my destiny." They kissed again and both laughed with joy, so happy in each other's company.

"It too I think was fate that led me to you and the orchards of my father's manor. When we cleared the orchard last year after I came home from School in Wroxeter, I had been studying Roman Goddesses

26

and found buried in the grass, a statue of Pomona the Goddess of Plenty and apple trees. Those trees must have been planted by the ancient Romans!

"I have another question for you my lady" he asked with a twinkle in his eyes, "This year after I graduated, I brought back with me some ancient Maps of the middle Sea, and old plans that showed how to construct a Roman Chariot. It will have a harness for two horses, and I have asked your father and mine, if it may be a wedding gift, so that you may arrive in grand style with your father to our wedding. Then you and I can return to Portmore Manor together, as man and wife."

Briefly her young eyes filled with a few tears of gladness, and she hugged him tightly and answered, "What a wonderful idea, the townsfolk will be agog, and I will be the proudest new wife the area has ever seen." She laughed again and asked mischievously, "Where can I get you a laurel wreath for your brow?"

Bride and Groom

Grainne and Cormac now mounted their horses, and turning to his fiancée, he said, "Does your horse have a name, he is as black as a birds wing, so you might call him Raven?"

She replied, "No name as yet, and the church would not like it I named him Odin." She laughed and agreed, "Raven it is, and a name for your chestnut coloured steed, what name have you chosen?"

He answered, "I am sure my mother would not object if I named him Bedwyr to honour my dear departed grandfather. "Then blissfully content in their own company, they cantered off to see his family and explain their wishes for the wedding ceremony, and they hoped that his baby sister Julia was not yet teething and could fill the church with her loud wails?

As they entered Portmore Manor, a groom was there to meet them and take their horses to the stables and he was asked to rub the horses down and set some feed before them. At the main door, his mother and baby sister were impatiently waiting to bid them sit a while and discuss the wedding plans, so they hugged both mother and child, and walked with them to the kitchen for some simple food, while baby Julia was fed. Moya began "If Abbott Peter is willing we should begin the ceremony at noon, to give time for guests to arrive who may have travelled some distance."

Both protested quietly so as not to wake Julia who was now contentedly asleep, but said in unison, "But we wanted a small wedding. Who are these guests, apart from our families, Captain Huw, the Abbott, brother Galen and the Earl of Chester's family? Cormac has not invited his recently graduated friends."

Moya responded after she had laid her baby in the cradle, "My husband feels that it would be good to include some of the investors of NEW DEVA TRADING COMPANY and their wives, and they may choose to bring you wedding gifts Afterwards, they can all join us for a wedding feast outside in our formal garden; most of them live in town houses within the fortress walls, and this setting would be new to them. There will be music from local players and our servants can join in the dancing, later on, sharing any food that has not been eaten. They will be provided with small beer or cider, on the grassed area by our orchards. Of course, you young lovers can slip away quite early after feast, Earl Edwin has arranged for you to stay the night elsewhere, is that agreeable'?

Reluctantly they both agreed, and then Moya wanted to talk about dresses for a maid of honour and a bridesmaid, Grainne said she had asked Violet, the oldest unmarried daughter of Earl Brocmale to be principle bridesmaid, who had agreed.

A somewhat nervous Cormac then sought out his father, but Skeggi had no practical advice about weddings, and wondered if he alone now needed to prepare a speech that was suited to a wedding day. Later he would talk to Earl Edwin and enquire about when his future father-in-law had married, many years ago.

At Your Service

The day of the wedding came all too soon for the ladies, who until yesterday had been still fussing about last minute touches to what they expected to be a perfect day that finally united the families of Earl Edwin and Sir Skeggi. An unexpected message from Chester magistrates was delivered by a uniformed rider with the crest of Chester on his cap badge He delivered a note to Ecclestone Manor advising the steward that it contained urgent news, to be read immediately by Earl Edwin.

Somewhat puzzled as to what this urgent news might be, he broke the wax seal, and having read the contents he sent for his daughter immediately, she came hurrying from her bedroom followed by her personal maid who had been setting Grainne's lustrous hair into a profusion of curls.

"It's that damned scoundrel, your cousin Rollo de Bretton, he has escaped from the prison in Snotingaham Castle, it is believed his uncle bribed the guards, and the prisoner escaped in a waiting boat on the nearby River Trent," snarled Edwin.

He continued, "Let us hope Rollo is not returning to Chester seeking revenge after his plan to claim our manor for his own failed. Do you recall the siege and how the Gunnarson family helped us catch him, and he was sent away to Goal? He always maintained that you and I had died at sea, those 4 years past."

Grainne shivered as she recollected that incident and was disturbed and anxious that nothing would spoil her wedding day, so they sent a word of warning to Portmore Manor. It was time for the grooms to prepare the chariot that would take Edwin and Grainne to the Church of St John the Baptist.

Two flat bottomed ferry boats were needed, one to take the chariot with Edwin and the bride, while the second boat took the horses and groom. Before arriving at the church, the groom harnessed the two horses to the wedding chariot, and father and daughter climbed aboard, and trotted sedately past the waving crowds of townsfolk, who stood amazed at the spectacle.

The bridegroom was waiting expectantly with the ornately garbed Abbott on the steps of the church. The town watch and extra armed guards were stationed at all the doors and paths to the church, having been alerted by the courts that an escaped prisoner may be in the vicinity. In the bell tower, a bowman had been stationed and was watchful and carried a hunting horn to give a warning blast to alert the congregation.

Unusually, Sir Skeggi was allowed to wear his double axe in his belt, and Earl Edwin wore a short sword. Cormac had the tarn helm fixed to his belt, explaining that it was ceremonial use only, and would not be worn in the church.

Next the Abbott and his small group of priests entered the church first carrying the cross and others within had alerted the musicians, who began to play a processional hymn. They were seen to be playing the shawm, fiddles, a rebec, a crwth, plus the trumpet, timbrel, and lute , while the choir of young altar boys sang.

ALONE AT LAST

Despite the concerns of the bride and groom's families, the wedding service ended without incident, and when the newlyweds left the church, both their fathers embraced them, and a small crowd cheered, some hoping for a shower of small coins to be tossed to them.

Lady Moya thanked the bridesmaids and complemented the musicians, eventually the wedding group made its way back to the river and the chariot. On guard there stood some of the town watch and the ferryman had decorated his boat with ribbons and some flowers for the couple and their chariot, while a second ferry waited for Sir Skeggi and Lady Moya, Earl Edwin and bridesmaid Violet. More craft had been hired to bring the important guests, while the Earl Brocmale and his wife had their official barge. As they set off for the short journey upstream to Portmore Manor, Bishop Peter and his priests chanted a farewell in plainchant style.

The happy bride and groom were alone at last except for the discrete old ferryman, and Cormac was bursting with pride to have such a beautiful wife at his side and whispered, "Your father has loaned me the keys to Ecclestone Manor and has thoughtfully invited all your servants and land workers families to join the celebrations at Portmore Manor, so we will be alone, except for a few guards."

The two of them were startled to see a bird perch on Cormac's shoulder, and Grainne exclaimed, "Is that Odin's raven, returned to you after these four years?"

Cormac answered, "You can now see him too?"

Then they both heard the once familiar noise of avian greeting *'hrokar, hrokar'*, that had meant a personal message between father and son. "Danger awaits you both at break of dawn tomorrow, Rollo and a small gang of escaped criminals intend to murder you."

Cormac then begged Odin's raven, "Take this same message to my father Skeggi Gunnarson, who follows us a little distance downstream'.

The raven croaked the reply, "Skeggi already knows Cormac; I gave him this message first." Taking no chances, Cormac asked the ferryman to row his boat more slowly and allow the other ferry with their parents on board to come closer and so arrive together.

Our young husband now turned to his new wife and spoke in low tones "We must be alert my love and not take any risks to the lives of ourselves or our family, but also not underestimate this crazed, vengeful cousin of yours. When I get you to our manor, I will immediately find Brother Kell's holy cards. They will show us how to overcome this terrible danger. My father and yours have much experience in armed combat, and how to employ stealth against an enemy."

The Wedding Feast

With the wedding celebrations of that afternoon and evening ahead, Cormac leaped onto the manor's landing stage calling for the watchtower guard, then the chariot and horses were led off the ferry, and next he reached out to help his wife alight. The specially decorated ferry moved a little upstream, to allow the other boats to have their passengers get off, and soon a small party of dignitaries and other guests clustered round the bride, offering polite compliments and a few men laughingly offered wedding night advice to Cormac, politely out of hearing of Grainne.

While the ladies escorted the bride to the manor, Earl Edwin and Sir Skeggi, called the Earl of Chester and Abbott Peter to one side to talk in private. Talking quickly and with little explanation, they alerted these men, to send word back to Chester with news that the escaped prisoner Rollo de Bretton had been observed by the manor watchtower to be making his way stealthily upstream on the opposite bank with an armed band of ruffians-armed bowmen were needed to arrive as secretly as possible to repel any attack. The men folk here should be alerted not to frighten the ladies, as these invaders would not arrive here until dusk.

So, the wedding feast began, and Abbott Peter gave thanks for the food, and for those who had skilfully prepared it. Cormac stood proud and tall and welcomed the guests, thanked his parents, and profusely thanked Earl Edwin for having such a beautiful daughter, the Abbott and his priests for a heart-warming service and pertinent homily- the latter words spoken in Latin. "My wife and I (a few cheers and laughs erupted) thank you for honouring us today, and we appreciate the many unexpected gifts you have generously and thoughtfully provided (at this point the guild members clapped and cheered)."

Then signalling the servants, he said, "Enjoy with us this splendid feast, and later those excellent musicians from our church will entertain you, and there is space for dancing! Please excuse me for one moment," he said. He signaled the steward, who brought forth a large bunch of special flowers saying, "These are offered with love to my mother Lady Moya, and chosen by my dear wife, a token of our great love for you. We have an abundance of wine and ale, not quite on the scale of the wedding at Cana." And so many toasts ensued.

"Our hard-working servants and tenants should not be neglected, so excuse us while we greet them." So, Cormac and his father took the path behind the manor to the trestle tables to serve their workers and take some extra ale and mead, asking them to drink sparingly.

They noted the preparations they had secretly requested- set against a fence were extra weapons- pitchforks, cudgels, daggers, scythes and sickles, a few bows and quivers of arrows, and some shields. The watchtower guards were also armed with bow and arrows, and spears, with the warning ram horn at the ready. Father and son returned to the feast, smiling, and speaking quietly to Edwin and Grainne. Later, a glorious sunset was slowly filling the sky.

The happy couple excused themselves from the feast to a chorus of mildly unsuitable comments from some of the more inebriated men, and a blushing Cormac replied "My dear wife needs to change out of her wedding clothes, as do I."

Once inside the manor Cormac explained to Grainne that there was an urgent need to consult Brother Kell's book of holy cards, and together they would look for guidance. Quickly retrieving the cards from their hiding place, they riffled through the cards waiting for a sign, and turning to his wife Cormac said, "I am so sorry my love that the expected attack by Rollo and his gang means that our wedding night must be postponed, and we need to have your father escort my mother and baby Julia to the safety of nearby Ecclestone Manor, some of his servants will go with them."

Meanwhile escaped prisoner Rollo and his 3 criminals have made their way upstream along the bank of the River Dee looking for a way to cross over to Portmore Manor unobserved. After 4 years in prison with no visitors and poor food, Rollo is now unkempt, bearded and a little unsound of mind, for in those lonely days and nights in his cell he had befriended a white mouse which he called Fred, sharing breadcrumbs and complaining bitterly to the creature about his unjust imprisonment. The gaoler had taken pity on him and provided a small cage for the rodent. Now enjoying freedom, Rollo carries the cage with Fred attached to his belt, which he had stolen from a washing line en route to Chester. His gang of 3 were all from the street of bellies, Beormingahām; convicted of thefts from hand carts, as far as Rollo could tell from their accents, their names were Vern O' The Mill, Peter Akimbo and Ron Rose. Fate or fortune favoured them, and they found a fisherman's boat and oars tied to a willow tree by the bank of the river. His henchmen, he discovered to his dismay had no weapons training, and were only used to using pointed sticks or a shovel, so sighing he decided not to trust them with a blade, but if their attack was discovered he would send them charging at his enemies while he stayed back with his bow and arrows aiming to kill Cormac and disappear like the coward he was. He had hopes that a servant recently dismissed for stealing would have met with a surly Portmore Manor groom (who had previously been briefly employed 4 years ago by Rollo), would leave the manor's kitchen door unlocked, this night.

As the sky darkened and the full blush of sunset tinted the landscape, the wedding guests said their thanks and farewells, and left in the waiting ferries that would take them back to Chester, the Earl of Chester's official barge was last to leave, and Rollo's invaders waited their chance to slip across the river a mile upstream. Their simple plan was to hide until nightfall in the copse of trees that formed a border with the manor's orchards, each had a small woollen blanket stolen from a shepherd's cottage outhouse, later they would find to their cost ,that these blankets were infested with ticks and maggots.

Our newlyweds had asked to be left alone and only be quietly summoned by their servants after midnight, to join the defence of their home. Together that evening they prayed for guidance, and finally one card seemed to glow and when turned over, the image was of a Saker falcon. Cormac uttered the holy invocation and that very bird flew in through the window hole where its covering of thin animal skin had moved aside in the wind, it settled on a roof beam.

Cormac said quietly, "Soon I may seem to be asleep, but through this bird I will soar above our lands and see with its keen eye, any movements of humans." But Grainne was alarmed, and he said, "Haveno fear, just hold my hand and feel the pulse in my wrist like Brother Galen showed us, and you will know I am fine."

The Saker falcon now perched on the shoulder of her husband. She felt him lie back with his eyes open and the bird launched itself out and as she watched, the bird soared gracefully into the sunset. She looked to the skies but now the falcon was but a speck, so she returned to periodically check the pulse of her comatose lover.

As for Cormac, the thrill of flight was almost overwhelming, but then he recalled the time four years past when he used the sparrow hawk card at sea to spot that dis-masted ship carrying a young woman alone and left adrift near Liuerpul, home of the pirate slavers. Saving Grainne and later her father had changed his life completely, and gaining the slavers pirate hoard of great wealth, had paved the way to their new life together. The light was fading fast and then through the eyes of his falcon, saw four figures leaving a boat and making their way towards the manor, swooping lower he perched on an oak tree, and watched three men he did not recognise as local, trailing behind a fellow- almost unrecognisable with a beard and commoners clothing, was Rollo! On his bidding the hawk soared into the skies once more and found a place to rest on the manor watchtower. So, he thought, our old enemy has returned, this time he will cause our families no more harm, and he deserves to die. The keen eyes of the bird saw the would-be invaders; take a path around the orchards into the woods behind and disappear into the undergrowth. Aha, he thought, your attack will be no surprise and we shall be ready for you and your ruffians.

THICK AS THIEVES

The Saker falcon returned to Grainne, perched on Cormac's chest, and vanished. She reached out to wake him, then he stirred, sat up and smiled "I had forgotten the joy of flying and seeing our home from the skies, but good fortune has favoured us, my love, for I have seen the wooded area where our attackers are hiding, hoping to surprise us under cover of the early dawn. Your foul cousin Rollo leads a band of 3 other scoundrels, so we must think of setting traps to surprise, impede and kill, or capture them."

Together they dressed in less colourful garb and joined his father who was waiting in the main hall, and who was told what had been discovered about the enemy. Grainne chose a small bow and a quiver of metal tipped arrows; Skeggi wore his double headed axe and held an old javelin. Small, covered lanterns were lit, and with the steward and some burly servants they began to move, one by one, leaving the lanterns behind they went through the door and around the moat to the stables and orchard. They saw the area was in part shadow cast by the manor; the rest was bathed in weak moonlight.

Dressed in dark hooded cloaks the defenders split up, some to alert the watchtower guards, others to hide in the barns by the orchards, and then let loose some pigs to forage for windfall apples in the orchard. Accompanied by his personal groom Cormac headed for the stables carrying his tarn helm, with his bronze axe in his belt, together with a wickedly sharp iron dagger. The groom carried a horse blanket and an apple for Cormac's horse Bedwyr and was surprised when he was handed two horse chestnuts still in their spiky shells. Speaking quietly, he told the puzzled groom to put the large seeds gently on the horse's back, and cover it with the blanket, fixing the blanket loosely with a leather girth.

The horse was quieted, and the top half of the stable door left open, then the nearby horse trough was carefully refilled with water and cow dung and pigs manure added liberally. Next, they moved back to the kitchen door and with some twine they rigged up the blackest metal pans they could spare and strung them between two small posts-the clanging noise would alert them if the attackers entered that way. Understanding a little, the groom chuckled- "serve 'em right," he whispered.

They entered the manor, closing but not locking the door, and then sat waiting in the darkness for the battle that was to come. After some time, they heard a noise of stealthy footsteps, and the light from a candle as the other surly groom (he had been previously employed by Rollo and later demoted by Earl Edwin) walked into the dark kitchen showing only the dim light of a few embers. He unlatched the door and waved his candle in the direction of the woods, and leaving the door open, crept away, only to be seized, his cries muffled with a rag, and then he was bound hand and foot, and shoved into a storage cupboard.

Companions in Misfortune

Our young trio of escaped prisoners dozed uncomfortably for a while when Ron woke the others, and they all began to itch from the flea bites. They looked over to their bullying leader Sir Rollo, (as they had been told to address him), and Vernon whispered to the others "Why are we here, so far from home, and why were we helped to escape, our sentence was only 3 months?"

They grumbled and thought sadly of the circumstances that had led them to be arrested. Peter squinted at his childhood friends and spoke longingly of the brothers and sister they had not seen-no visitors allowed. How much he missed his father who had been lost at sea. Ron spoke of the good times after village school lessons provided by a benevolent local priest; when class had finished for the day, they would annoy the neighbours with little pranks until called in for supper. Often, they would pretend to be heroes from the Old Testament.

Together they sighed and Vernon said, "Remember James who led our small gang that included Malcolm and studious Mick- the youngest by a few months. It was Mick's silly idea to climb on that miserly farmers cart, while he was delivering to a customer's back door, and then push the cart behind a fence, and pelt him with bird's eggs. He had us three arrested, the swine, the others ran off, and we had done nothing really wrong."

Ron answered, "What rotten luck, and so were those eggs!" He grinned mischievously. "Despite our parents and the priest pleading leniency for us, I never expected us to be taken before the magistrates."

Peter answered, "Yes, the older villagers were tired of our light-hearted escapades, and demanded a custodial sentence. That was harsh and unjustified, but the magistrate chose to make an example of us. The Beormingahām prisons were full after that apprentice's riot, and we got shipped off to far away

Snottingherham. They all agreed they had no quarrel with the owner of the manor and had no wish to be killed to suit Sir Rollo's plans of vengeance, and when told to attack they would shout loudly and get captured, returning to prison was the safer option!

Now Sir Rollo woke, scratched himself absently and walked over to his scruffy trio, "Time for action my lads," he said, doubting they would be much use except as a distraction while he trounced his enemies who would soon be grovelling for mercy. They must die he thought, and I will claim my inheritance at last! So, they made their way through the woods and down into the orchards, where Peter promptly fell over a pig asleep under the trees, with its belly full of windfall apples and Peter was knocked unconscious! "No delays, we must leave him for now and recover him when we leave with our loot," muttered Rollo angrily.

There's Many a Slip

Sir Skeggi and his steward crouched under the large table in the kitchen and waited patiently for noise of the metal pots and pans to sound their warning, Our Viking hefted his favourite double-bladed axe which he had lovingly kept razor sharp, while his steward held a large meat clever at the ready.

Above them, peering through her window was Skeggi's new daughter in law, her bow and arrows ready at hand. With the armed servants hidden on the approaches to the manor, and Cormac ready to don the tarn helm, the invaders would be caught totally by surprise, and vastly outnumbered!

As dawn's fiery fingers broke over the landscape, the warmth brought a mist rolling in from the river and into the estate, reducing visibility for everyone, but an encouragement for Rollo's band of fugitives, who hope to enter unobserved. Ron and Vernon slowly advanced ahead of their leader, holding stout cudgels they had cut from tree branches a little earlier. They were now angry that their friend Peter had callously been left among the pigs on the dew-soaked ground, and if not for Sir Rollo's weapons, they might have attacked him instead. Approaching the open kitchen door, Vernon tripped on the mist hidden warning device of metal pans which clanked loudly, and Ron was scared out of his wits when a tall Viking strode out to face him, axe in hand and fell backwards losing his cudgel. Sir Rollo was shaking in fear and quickly turned about and ran for the stables, hoping to ride away from capture. He muttered an oath and then laughed to see a horse's head peering out at him.

Swiftly he opened the bottom half of the stable door and his terror enabled him to leap onto the back of the horse. He was about to gallop away, when the horse began to rear and buck violently, not yet grasping the reins, he fell headfirst into the horse trough. He attempted to get out and run away, but an invisible hand pushed him spluttering back into the evil smelling water, and he felt his jaw almost crack as a blow from the flat of a weapon which sent him unconscious.

Cormac took off the tarn helm, and with the help of his father, hauled a smelly Rollo onto the path. The steward came forward with the end of the twine with the clanking pots still attached, and bound Rollo hand and foot; he looked a sorry sight, as a bruise began to blacken his jaw. Workers began to come forward from their hiding places, farming weapons no longer needed, and two of them carrying the struggling form of abandoned Peter, He was doused with trough water to awaken him, which he did with a splutter, and feebly asked where his friends might be?

Cormac looked him in the eye and said, "They are safe over there, whoever they are." Peter looked around, and said, "Do not harm them; we are childhood friends, bullied by that evil man, Sir Rollo, into attacking the manor. He meant to kill you.

Vernon in the kitchen doorway over there, and Ron being held down by your men never intended to harm anyone. So, I beg you to be lenient, we were unjustly imprisoned for a foolish prank, back in our village. How far is it to Beormingahām?

Normality Restored

The groom came over and asked Cormac to visit the stables to calm the horse, and remove the blanket covering the hidden spiky horse chestnut shell, their plan had worked perfectly, and no-one had been harmed. All involved were invited into the kitchen and given a hearty breakfast cut from a side of bacon, and congratulated on the teamwork, and then they happily returned to their families, or to prepare for the day's work ahead. By now daylight had returned and the watchtower horn sounded two blasts as a group of horsemen were approaching the manor. It was the magistrate and the town watch, and a stranger bearing the flag of Snottingherham, come to reclaim the prisoners. Bound and gagged, Sir Rollo was escorted down the path to meet them, and the flag bearer handed a warrant to Sir Skeggi proclaiming, "I am Captain Hewitt sent from the prison, here with this re-arrest warrant for the 4 escaped prisoners, but I see only one. "Earl Edwin with Esquire Cormac by his side now addressed the captain. "You are most welcome, and we gladly hand over this scoundrel, Sir Rollo de Bretton to your custody, he was captured attempting to enter this manor and kill us, but he was easily overpowered. His companions babbled something to my servants who confronted them in our fields, but they ran off and we have since noticed a small boat is missing, so we assume they have absconded, "Cormac offered helpfully.

Lady Grainne now came forward and said, "You must be weary, and the hour is early, but I am sure our cook could provide some food and drink. "The captain and his companions smiled, and he replied graciously "Thank you for your kind offer but this sorry villain must be returned to Chester, while others continue the search for the three miscreants- O'The Mill, Akimbo and Rose."

So, the officials turned their mounts and trotted off, with their tethered prisoner made to run behind them. Earl Edwin then returned to Ecclestone, to collect Lady Moya and baby Julia and relate the excitement of this early morning, then bring them back to Portmore Manor.

Cormac and his father now went over to a locked stable where the three captured prisoners were hidden from view. They greeted the sorry group, untied their limbs, and Cormac told them, " We mean you no harm and believe your tale of injustice, we have sent Sir Rollo back to prison with an escort, and have told the magistrate and his yeoman of the watch that you ran away and sailed off in a stolen boat, now let us tend to your flea bites and any other injuries, and there is still some hot bacon, fresh bread and small beer to restore your spirits."

So, the three friends were taken to the kitchen, and over breakfast were asked to explain how they came to be imprisoned, then Peter, Ron and Vernon took turns to scoff the food and tell their sorry tale. Peter asked politely if there was more bread, but only yesterday's loaf remained, so that was toasted over the fire for him, and spread generously with butter, while Ron asked for and was given apple juice. They could not believe how lucky they had been to be treated so well. Earl Edwin smiled and said, "I too know what it means to be locked up and held for ransom by pirates"

They looked at him open mouthed, "crumbs" they said in unison "Pirates!"

DREAMS

Cormac looked at the three friends and said, "You have had a bad start in your lives; try and put it all behind you and follow your dreams, if you have any. Once I lived in a poor village in Ireland, look at me now!"

They stared at him, a little alarmed and amazed, and haltingly Ron said, "I was once told in school about a man from ancient Greece who could fly, someday in the future I believe men will make flying machines."

Vernon gazed around him and said, "One day I hope a descendant of mine will plan grand houses like these."

Peter was last to speak saying, "When I see lightning in the sky, maybe we can make our own lightning, not to burn and destroy, but provide bright light instead of these lanterns."

It was now Cormac's turn to be surprised, and mused, "I have travelled far, and have plans to trade in the lands of the Greeks, but your dreams have astounded me."

Their benefactor stood up and told them he would think for a while and consult his father-in-law, as to how we might help you get back home- saying, "Is it in Beormingahām, many leagues south of here?"

Tears filled their eyes, and they bowed clumsily and muttered, "Blimey, that's rear-lly great."

Grainne reckoned their honeymoon had been postponed long enough, so her father agreed to move in to Portmore Manor for a few days. The newlyweds collected their horses and some changes of clothes and set off to Ecclestone Manor to begin their new life as man and wife. It was only a short ride, but they had so much to talk about but also were more than ready to discover the delights that each might bring to the other that night. They ate a light supper, thoughtfully provided by her father's cook, and decided to forego the flasks of wine, and bid the servants not to waken them next morning, unless there was an emergency. Cormac said to her softly, "It is strange that we really hardly know each other, with me being mostly away these last four years getting a degree, while you have managed your father's household."

Her answer was, "At the beginning, those first two years apart seemed like a lifetime, and then I remembered that it was destiny that you rescued me, and we fell in love. Our family will forever be in your debt after you risked your life to save my father from the pirate slavers, and now our dearest wish has been granted, and our families are now become one."

Their first night together, alone at last, was very special to them as they explored their nakedness, until urgency overpowered their reticence and they succumbed to each other's needs and were delighted to discover how natural their lovemaking became and the soft languor that followed. With much youthful energy the delights continued until they fell into a dreamless sleep of exhaustion, in a tangle of limbs. The next morning Cormac was awake first and gazed at Grainne's unadorned beauty, and marvelled at what further nights together might bring, and a little relieved that Brother Galen had prescribed a natural herbal potion of gossypol seeds, which prevented an early pregnancy.

Ship Ahoy

As they ate a late breakfast, satisfying a different hunger, Cormac smiled tenderly at his wife and said, "Last night we learned some marvellous new skills that we will never share with another, but being part of wealthy families means we have need of more life skills. Our time together on the ship of Captain Huw taught me how to be a common sailor, but our future trading plans require new abilities needed on a long voyage."

Grainne replied, "Like Ruth the Moabite in the Bible, I will go where you go, for you are my life and my love."

Cormac grinned and said, "I hope you will enjoy my little surprise, then."

She laughed and said, "You mean more surprises than last night?"

His face turned a little mysterious and he took her hand and said, "Come with me."

He slowly led her outside to where a servant held the reins of their horses, now hitched up to a wagon covered by sailcloth. With a flourish he removed the cover to reveal a small sailboat, its mast lying flat, and two oars.

She looked a little taken aback at first, her mind returning to when she was rescued at sea in a similar small boat, four years ago, but then realised that a sailing lesson might be involved. "Are we going sailing on the River Dee?" she inquired.

"I was thinking of somewhere a little more private and calmer," he said. "Cook has prepared a meal of cheese, fresh bread, some sweet apples and a flask of cider. Your steward and your maid also have food and will come with us on a smaller cart to attend to us and guard our belongings while we go sailing."

She replied, "So we will not be alone then?"

Her questions were answered when after a few leagues, they arrived at the hamlet of Dodlestone, and took a path through woodlands to see the blue waters of a quiet lake with an island having what looked like a fisherman's hut.

At the edge of the lake was a small landing stage and a fallen log to sit upon, and it was here they left behind her steward and maid, who handed her mistress the basket of provisions, and two large towels. Cormac and the steward hauled the sailing boat from the wagon, dragged it down a slip way and launched the vessel, while Grainne held onto the mooring rope. Cormac gingerly climbed aboard and set about hoisting the mast, then helped his wife aboard too. The rope was taken aboard and coiled neatly by Grainne, who trying not to rock the boat, sat down, while her husband took the oars, waved to the servants saying, "We will be back here at dusk."

And so, began their first voyage as man and wife. Throughout the morning they enjoyed a light breeze, and the sail was hoisted, speeding their travel to the far side of the island, while Cormac explained how to sail into the wind, to turn about and not get knocked overboard, to raise and lower the sail. With the sail lowered, they took turns to use the oars, and there was much laughter as both got splashed a little, and Cormac could not help noticing how her dress now clung enticingly to her bosom...

Splashing Out

As the sun climbed in the sky above them, they decided to seek some shade on the island, so Cormac rowed them steadily towards the fisherman's jetty, and then with oars backing water, glided them gently to dry land. While her husband held onto a mooring post, Grainne got ready to leap onto the jetty not realising that the island had long been abandoned, and then the wooden jetty just crumbled, and she tumbled into the lake. Cormac stifled a laugh, but when she began to laugh, he joined in too, and after tying the boat to the post, slid into the water as well, and in the shallows, lifted her in his strong arms and waded ashore. For a while they lay on the grassy bank to dry out in the hot sun, then thinking of food, he waded back into the shallows to reclaim their feast. They squelched along the path to the fisherman's hut, and found it to be mostly clean and dry, as someone had placed a woven cover over the smoke hole in the roof. There was a door of sorts, but it had seen better days, and sagged forlornly, "This will suffice and keep us private and sheltered from the breeze," he said.

While ever practical, his beloved replied, "We need to get out of these wet clothes and leave them on bushes to dry in the sun." He responded enthusiastically (*hmmm, too enthusiastically* she thought, blushing a little), but nevertheless obliged him, while he grinned and helped her, his mind re-living last night's naked adventures.

They opened the cloth wrappings of the food, and set aside the flask of cider, "I see your appetite has not diminished," she remarked, and noticing his groin area continued "and not just for food I see."

He noticed a stiffening of the tips of her breasts and happily forgot the repast, while she lay back and he came to her, this time with a greater degree of control and wave upon wave of passion engulfed them. Later they remembered their discarded clothing still needed to dry, so Cormac dashed out to the bushes and laid out their garments to dry, then returned to satisfy the other hunger, sharing the bread, cheese and ripe apples, and gratefully noticed two small, sweet honey flavoured cakes .Then they shared the cider and dozed contentedly in each other arms. A cool breeze wafted through the door and woke them, and they saw streaks of sunset colour the skies, so Cormac raced outside and was delighted to find their clothing had become dry. As they dressed, he murmured in her ear, "We must do this again, soon my love."

At which she laughed and said, throatily, "You mean sailing, of course."

Searching for a large branch, he reached over the broken jetty and pulled the boat nearer to shore, before hoisting up his hose and paddling to take the mooring rope off the post. Helping Grainne back into the boat, he shoved off with the oars, and raised the sail and rounded the island, and sighted the servants lying fast asleep on the grass some distance from the slipway.

They each took an oar and gently prodded the servants awake, who began to stammer apologies, only to be told by their mistress, "We have had a wonderful experience, the sun shone brightly, and we enjoyed our midday meal after sailing to the end of the lake and sheltered in the hut. We hope you had a pleasant day, excused from your normal duties."

Planning a Future

A fine spring afternoon at Portmore Manor saw Cormac, Grainne, Edwin, Skeggi, Moya Brother Galen all sat around a large wooden table covered in charts, plans of shipbuilding, and monetary accounts, when the Earl glanced around the small group and remarked, "I still cannot believe that a year has passed by and we have made little progress with our great venture the NEW DEVA TRADING COMPANY."

Cormac responded complaining, "Our shareholders, especially Chester Guilds, have been too cautious and slow in depositing the funds that give them shares in the company. We need that capital to commission a new Carvel-built trading vessel, that will allow us to trade first with Brittany, and hire their experienced sailors so we may venture beyond the Pillars of Hercules and into the Middle Sea."

Sir Skeggi joined in the discussion. "Reports from Captain Huw are most encouraging, and he is happy that the new silver penny coins are common currency from the land of the Friesians and Aquitaine down to the Southern Visigoths and far off Naples."

Brother Galen encouraged the assembly by advising, "Our Pope St Sergius the 1st comes from the island of Sicily in the Middle Sea, and our Saxon and Celtic Monasteries send delegates, gifts and tithes overland and then by sea to Rome, the centre of our Christian faith', so the route is quite well travelled. The company would be well rewarded by many Abbotts if we chose to carry such a cargo."

Moya and Grainne offered practical advice with Moya saying, "These plans sound wonderful, but we need to be firm with these sluggard investors, and advise them that no shares, means no profit, and we are prepared to close membership to those who have not paid in good coin by Easter! Furthermore, before we have bought a new trading vessel, some of this party needs to charter Captain Huw's latest ship, *the Curlew* to sail to Brittany and conduct some trade to gain first-hand experience of cargo tonnage and small crews."

At this, Cormac stood up and applauded the ladies, saying, "My dear wife and my mother speak good sense. I propose we should make both Joint Company Treasurers. It would also be prudent to nominate Lord Brocmale, Earl of Chester, to be our Leader to encourage those that waver in their resolve?

A number of voices could now be heard commenting on recent ideas, so Earl Edwin brought the group to order saying, "I call upon Brother Galen to make a written record and I nominate him as Company administrator. If we are now in agreement, we will all sign our names or marks to this document he will provide, and copies will be presented to our first meeting of Shareholders in the NEW DEVA TRADING COMPANY!"

All present raised their right hands in agreement, and Brother Galen spoke a blessing on the venture that would benefit the community and Holy Church.

ANNIVERSARY

Our young married couple wondered if any family or friends would remember that they had been married one year tomorrow. Regular lovemaking had necessarily been curtailed as running Ecclestone Manor for Grainne was time consuming now that the orchards and vineyards of this manor and Portmore Manor were producing many fruits in season and attempts at wine making had meant considerable supervision.

As for Cormac, he was busy with meetings with the Chester Guilds, and taking opportunities to go aboard other trading vessels, to see their cargoes, and note what goods they exported from Chester and the surrounding area.

For the lovebirds, time together was precious, and they both needed to be aware of each other's needs, particularly as Cormac now understood that his wife was sometimes unwell or irritable resulting from her 'monthly course'. So, they devised a private signal while in company, of when holding hands, the silent request for a conjugal visit was if the partner's hand was lightly stroked in the middle of the palm of the others hand. A responding two strokes meant yes, but one stroke back meant no. This was confirmed by a nod or shake of the head, and it had worked well during the last 6 months. Also, Brother Galen's supply of gossypol seeds potions was not regularly obtainable, which meant abstinence.

During family meals at both manors, heated exchanges were frequent, with opposing views as to the risk to finances, health, and lives! Finally, a compromise was reached, when Cormac proposed that he and Brother Galen join the crew of Captain Huw's ship that was soon bound for Brittany. His father demanded that he join them so that his son would have time to master the navigation skills he would teach him.

This was reluctantly accepted by all, and Moya thought privately that she would be distraught if harm came to her men. Galen advised them that the company's first contract was from a group of Bishop's to deliver a strongbox of coin, gifts, and messages to the Holy Father in Rome. They would deliver the tithes and offerings to the Abbey of Saint Meen in Brittany, who would arrange for an armed caravan mustered at the Monastery of St John that would deliver it to Rome. Abbott Chad would welcome them, although papal news was that he had been ill.

Grainne and Cormac travelled to Chester with Sir Skeggi to meet captain Huw and plan the course to Brittany. They all met at the palace of Lord Brocmale and were joined by Abbott Peter who offered prayers for the success of the first voyage of the NEW DEVA TRADING COMPANY, in which he held shares.

He brought the most recent news from Brittany, known locally as the Kingdom of Dumnonia, ruled by King Alain the second who had recently succeeded his father King Judicael.

Trading Places

Huw, Captain of the *Merlin*, advised that the most popular goods traders bought from Brittany were salt, woollen goods and cloth, dried and salted fish, a drink made from fermented pears, fine gold brooches, and glass bowls. He further suggested that Cormac's roman-style chariot would be a rarity in the lands of the middle sea, but would also make a fine gift or bribe to King Alain of Brittany and the Visigoth ruler of Cartagena? Was it possible to have copies made, but in parts for assembly by his crew? The Earl of Chester thought this was a magnificent idea, and he was willing to hire more craftsmen from the Guilds to make this possible, but they should be manufactured in secret and only parts of the plans shown to workers, not the whole design?

Cormac responded, "I agree about the secrecy of design, as only a few monks and scholars of ancient lore would know of this, but my chariot is quite unadorned and practical, we need some extra features like fine leather harness, gilding and ornate metal work. Also, maybe some soft woollen padding dyed purple, fit for Kings would be a good investment?"

Grainne had been quiet until now and spoke up, "If this gift is for a King, maybe we should include some finely fletched arrows and sturdy bows that our region is famed for."

Sir Skeggi added "The strongboxes of coin for the Pope will need trustworthy armed guards, good Christians who will defend it with their lives until it is safely transferred to St John's Monastery and become the Brittany Abbott's responsibility. Our Abbot Peter will enlist the soldiers, but I would like to test their fighting skills before agreeing."

Brother Galen and a trusted scribe would make a written record for future meetings of shareholders of their Trading Company, and commission a highly decorated manuscript signed with Abbot Peter's Seal of Office, as proof of their Trading Credentials.

Earl Brocmale spoke as they began to leave the meeting. "I have news. My eldest daughter, Violet, is betrothed to Adolphus Viscount of the Wirral estates. I believe he went to the same seat of learning as you young Cormac?"

A chill ran down Cormac's spine and he stood rigid for a moment his face turning pale, but he soon recovered his composure, unnoticed except by his wife. Returning home by the town's river ferry, she asked quietly, "Is there something troubling you about the news that Violet is betrothed? Shouldn't you be happy for her? She is a good friend to me and being plain of features she thought her fate would be in a Nunnery."

In an undertone, for his father was with them, he replied, "This is terrible news; I will say more until we are alone, but he was a bully when I was a student at Wroxeter Abbey."

OLD ENMITES

'**S**keggi left the town ferry and Grainne and her husband continued to Ecclestone Manor and paid the ferryman his fee. They strolled to a quiet spot and sat on a log and Cormac was ready to reveal what his experience of Adolphus had been, while they had been at Wroxeter Abbey School together.

He said, "Have you ever taken an immediate dislike to someone after only a short acquaintance? It was like that with me on my first day as a new pupil. Adolphus was two years ahead of me and already a prefect, and my classmates were already in fear of him.

From a distance he seemed so perfect, angelic almost, with his blonde curls, cornflower blue eyes and he had a tall, sturdy frame, much better dressed than the other students. But if we think eyes are the windows of the soul, he was soul-less.

He could turn almost purple with rage for no reason, and he carried an ornate carved stick with a handle of walrus bone. When he thought no-one was looking, he would strike a smaller first year lad at the back of the knee causing him to fall over yelping in pain, then he and his cronies would laugh and call out 'clumsy oaf'. Of course, I was nearer to his height and build and stood out from the crowd with my red hair.

"For the next two years he tried to make my life a misery, but I told no-one, as I discovered that the teacher in charge of outdoor activities was his uncle, who indulged his antics. Those pupils caught fighting were sent home for a term, and I did not want my father returning with me, demanding blood!

"During those dark times I fervently wished for my father's tarn helmet to spy on my enemy's misdeeds or escape his creepy gaze. I learned to wear a cap to cover my hair, and to stoop a little to seem smaller, and avoid the places he frequented after school hours.

My chance came when I was allowed home for Easter, and asked Brother Galen after Good Friday mass if he might supply me a remedy for irregular bowel movements, which he kindly did providing a small phial but, warning me most sternly that to only take the smallest spoonful when needed. Easter was over all too soon and I begged permission from my father to borrow the tarn helm, so that I might find a quiet place to study in my noisy school, full of distractions."

Listening intently Grainne replied, "I did wonder about those bruises you often came home with, but expected they were obtained on the playing field. So, what did you do in retaliation?"

In answer, Cormac continued, "Final year students were allowed to leave school after classes but must return before sundown, otherwise the gates would be locked and any absent students at next morning's roll call would be punished severely, even expelled. But down the years students had found ways to leave by scaling the high walls, or finding gaps in the fences, even built short tunnels! A cruel gang of oldest students would waylay a returning chap and force him to pay them to re-enter after sundown, and this was the trick of Adolphus and his gang."

EXPULSION

Cormac resumed his tale. "It was the last week of term and retrieving the magic helmet from my locked box covered by books and clothing, I waited until classes finished for the day and with a group of friends, followed Adolphus and his cronies out of the school gates and took the narrow lane into the nearby village. There were some stalls that sold small cakes and honey, and others that had caps and scarves and socks that pupils often needed to buy when their own had been torn, stolen, or flung up into tall trees as a prank. The last building was a tavern that sold simple food, small beer, fermented apple juice, or cheap wine, a favourite among the final year's students, and at the rear was a shed with a few beds for assignations with willing serving maids.

"I idled the evening away with my classmates, until it was approaching sunset. Muttering some excuse about having only small coins for a drink, I entered the tavern, to see my enemy and his friends enjoying some dubious meat pies and many empty tankards lay on the stained trestle table while Adolphus had a buxom wench on his lap.

"I greeted Adolphus and bowed saying, "I shall miss your prowess on the sporting field good sir, you have made your uncle proud. So, may I buy you a farewell drink?"

Adolphus stood up, swaying a little and responded, "You may buy me and my friends a drink, and be quick fetching it, we can't wait to leave and join our rightful place in this land, serving our glorious King in his palace, army or his courts."

His three companions smirked and cheered their leader, thumping the table and shouting, "Girls for us too!"

"Only too happy to treat you fine fellows," I said, and signalling the tavern owner said, "Four of your best ales for these young graduates, I shall bring them over myself. "Soon the foaming drinks were poured, and a greasy tray was provided, then with my back to the gang I removed the phial from my tunic and liberally dosed each tankard with Galen's purgative.

First I served his cronies , then went back for the last tankard, this time adding the rest of the phial into the ale, faking a downcast smile I passed the tankard over to Adolphus, saying "A toast to your future as leaders of our land -down in one if you dare!"

Later all four bullies began to suffer painful stomach cramps and headed for the crowded privy, two of his cronies did not make it, having to wait for other customers, so shat themselves. The services of the wenches long forgotten, Adolphus and his friend ran into the nearby woods, straight into brambles and nettles, and a while later began to crawl out onto a field.

This was the chance I had been waiting for, slipping on the tarn helm; I knocked the first two unfortunates unconscious and tied them up. Gathering more thin rope, I crossed the field and silently reached my last two victims, feebly crawling on soiled hands and knees, removing the carved stick from Adolphus I thrashed both of them, and struck both heads with such a blow the cane snapped in two, and they too fell unconscious. Trussing them both up, I carried them one by one and dumped them into the tavern's pig pen. It was empty as the boar and sows were kept in a warm shed. Next morning all four were expelled.

Grainne laughed and then said seriously, "I must warn Lady Violet."

"We must be careful how we deal with Adolphus; he could be dangerous," murmured Grainne, thoughtfully. She continued, "Do you regret how you treated him, causing his expulsion from your school?"

Now it was Cormac's turn to be thoughtful and he considered his reply, finally saying, "He was a bully who made lives a misery for so many younger students, and had become casually brutal, with no-one to oppose him. For his own sake, and for the reputation of our school, he needed a sharp lesson, and the tarn helm gave me that opportunity, so no-one saw me. You know that Violet's father, Earl Brocmale, went to that same school, so I could advise him to enquire about Adolphus as a prospective husband. I will reluctantly give him my opinion, but only if he asks me."

An area of flat grassland lay between the river Dee and the town walls, its shape seen from the Castle resembled an eye, so the locals named it Rood Eye, and it was occasionally used for horse races and training the guards employed by the magistrates to defend the city. Sir Skeggi had been given the onerous task of improving the guards fighting skills and training new recruits.

Cormac had often thought of trying out his chariot driving skills, but there was not another chariot to race against him. Maybe when the new trading company had built a few chariots for future trading, they could be put through their paces before being disassembled to go aboard ship? Hmmm he thought, *maybe try only one at a time for secrecy, they will be a valuable asset'*.

Thinking ahead to the trading voyage he was planning, Cormac realised his own fighting skills needed improvement, having never faced a trained soldier, so he would ask his father if he might join the new recruits in their training. Skeggi and the Captain of the Guard were standing by the fortress wall and had some shields, swords, and spears on the grass, nearby in a large chest there were stored a few axes and clubs. Scattered on the grass were training swords of wood, also spear hafts with no blade, and a few paces towards the river a circle had been made using stones.

Out from gate leading into Bridge Street trooped a motley crew of raw recruits, some more smartly dressed, others wearing their farm workers clothes and a trio bringing up the rear of the column, encouraged by a few kicks and light blows from sticks. Cormac Gunnarson burst out laughing, and turning around, his father did also- it was the three hapless friends who had escaped from Snotingaham prison, set free by Earl Edwin, but now re-captured. Ron Rose, Peter Akimbo and Vern O'The Mill had obviously been apprehended trying to find their way home to Bereminghame.

Once more Sir Skeggi took pity on the trio and spoke to John O'Saltney, the Sergeant of the Guard. "I know these men, John, out of work and hungry they worked in my fields at Portmore Manor, but were useless, so we allowed them to find their way home. If there is a fine, I will pay it; just release them into my care."

The three detainees fell to the ground and grasped Sir Skeggi's legs, sobbing and moaning saying, "Youm trooly a saint, yer majesty, our mam's will bless you and loit undreds of candles for a loif toime of praiyin, we are your umbel sevants."

Raw Recruits

Cormac joined his father and offered to give some help to the eternally grateful but hapless three lads, by showing them some simple arms drills, and walked over with them to collect some wooden training weapons. Vern was the tallest, so he was given a spear haft, while Peter Akimbo had poor eyesight and so was provided with a short sword. Ron

Rose seemed the most agile and was rewarded with a club with a leather thong to go around his wrist which he immediately began to swing wildly, just missing his friend Peter.

Cormac chose another spear haft for himself and told them to follow him to the stone circle, explaining this was just practising and not to seriously hurt each other, or him! He said, "Listen to me carefully, tell no-one you are escaped prisoners and agree to admit to anyone who asks that you ran away from home to see the world."

The trio looked at him wide-eyed and said in chorus, "Yes mister, when do we get some food?"

Cormac had to turn away to stifle a chuckle, and then told them, "You must learn to defend yourselves. If you prove adept in wooden weapons use, you will be fed, and provided with a basic uniform, training with real weapons comes later. Now, you O'The Mill go back to the walls and bring me a shield. "He sighed and gazed at them, *this could be a long task,* he thought.

"Which one of you would like to join me in the combat ring?" he asked. So, Vern and Ron stepped back a pace, leaving Peter looking as if he had volunteered. "Brave lad Akimbo, that means that your friends will be fighting each other."

A town guard who had been watching was commanded to bring over two leather breastplates, one of which he showed Akimbo how to fasten. Next Cormac picked up the oval shield and showed Akimbo where to place his left arm through the inner handle to hold the shield. He said, "Normally you would also wear a helmet, but that comes later if and when you use real weapons, instead of this sword, you might have an angon (lance)."

"Look at me, and pretend I am an enemy or robber, but have no shield, only a pole, so defend yourself." Peter peered at Cormac and holding his shield to protect his chest, stepped close with his sword to confront the enemy, and promptly started hopping around in pain, for his adversary had jabbed his foot with the pole.

"Cor Blimey, bloody flippen hell, why did you do that, sir?"

Cormac called out to Vern and Ron who were watching and laughing, "See lads, the shield is not just for protecting the upper body, and remember if your enemy has a longer weapon, don't get up close to him. 'Now Step out of the combat ring Akimbo, that is something you will remember for the future, and remove the breastplate and pass the shield to Rose."

Turning to speak to the other two lads Cormac said," 'Now it's your turn Ron Rose and Vern O'The

Mill, in this combat ring, forget you are friends, and pick up a shield each and put on the leather breastplates."

Vern looked at Ron and said, "Don't worry, this pole is not going to hurt your feet."

Ron replied, "If I swing at your head, just duck."

CIRCLE OF FRIENDS

A small crowd now gathered, including townsfolk on the walls above, to enjoy free entertainment, and they even took sides! Cormac advised the combatants, "Before you begin, if you fall out of the circle, your opponent has won. If you cry ENOUGH, you have lost, so no playacting, I am watching you."

Voices from the crowd shouted, "Hey beanpole, give the fellow with the club a good whacking." Others called out, "Break his pole with your swinging club." But to no avail, the pair just shuffled around.

Ron Rose started a bit of a ducking and dancing movement, hoping to avoid any prods from Vern, who then tried to trip Ron by striking the back of his friend's knee. Akimbo was silent nursing his aching foot, and the two in the circle began to droop under the weight of their shields, so Vern winked at Ron and mouthed something quietly, then the crowd saw them leap at each other, bounce back, and both fall out of the circle. The crowd hissed and booed, and some threw mouldy apples at them.

Cormac raised his hand for silence, "These are just beginners with no weapons experience, but I see the tiny evidence of tactics, so I declare dancing Rose the victor." More boos and a few slow hand claps began, but with threats from the guards, the onlookers dispersed.

Turning to the trio he said, "Not a bad start for lads who have never seen a weapon. The guards will escort you to their barracks, where you will be bathed to remove the grime and sweat of days spent in the hedges and fields. I will have your clothing washed, dried and mended."

The trio almost replied in unison protesting, "But we had a bath at Christmastide, Master."

Putting on his most stern face, and speaking slowly and loudly, Cormac raised his training pole threateningly, and warned them, "The first one of you to complain again in my presence will be beaten with this. Be off with you, I shall visit you later today and inspect your miserable bodies for the slightest speck of dirt before you put on your cleaned clothing. No food until then."

"Bloody hells teeth," said Peter in a whisper. "Heem be wurst than me old mam', always inspecting the back of me neck and insoide me ears."

Calling out to the Guard Captain he told him to escort the trainees back to barracks, then in an undertone instructed him, "Have a barber cut their hair and use the old Tepidarium bath that the Romans left behind. Give them a scrubbing brush and some of that strong Viking soap, then douse them thoroughly in cold rainwater. I shall be back before noon hour with Sir Skeggi. Have you any old much mended uniforms that we can borrow?"

Daily Bread

Akimbo sighed, remembering the fresh hearth cakes that his mother used to cook on a hot stone. He had watched her make them, using her special blend of ground oats and barley (she called it maslin), then adding a little liquid. The water from the village pump was not drinkable unless you were really thirsty, so she would use some small beer, then knead the mixture it into dough and cook it for as long as she could recite the Lord's Prayer seven times. They would drink the rest of the small beer, sometimes dipping the cakes into it, and he especially loved the brown burnt bits which, because of drinking the beer, he called them toast.

Ron and Vern told him to be quiet, but their mouths watered, as they had yet to be fed, but now their skin no longer itched, but stung a little from the soap and scrubbing. After having had a bath together, their hands and feet felt smooth, and their hair no longer fell over their eyes. It had been fun splashing each other until the guard had come in, made them stand, and poured cold water over them, and then given squares of sack cloth to dry them.

An old women servant came in carrying coarse bread, some freshly churned butter, and a crumbly cheese, so the lads, still waiting for some clothing hastily wrapped the sack cloth around their genitals, she cackled showing only a few teeth and said, "Sir Skeggi has sent me with this food, and by the look of you, you need feeding, but one of you needs a bigger cloth." At this, Vern blushed. "I will be back soon with some bowls of hot broth," she said and hobbled off.

Ron rushed over to the food and began to devour it in large mouthfuls, quickly followed by the other two lads. Peter Akimbo said wistfully, "Is there any toast?" The broth then arrived, and they drained the bowls.

A guard came with their clothes, and they saw the rips and tears had been mended, so they dressed quickly in case younger females came along. Another guard came and escorted them back to the Rood Eye, and Sir Skeggi and Cormac were waiting for them. Sir Skeggi inspected the trio and shook his head wearily saying, "My son tells me that you are too unskilled in bearing weapons to be of any use to our town guard, so how might you be of use to us, and worthy of being fed?"

Vern spoke up, "Us three is reelly graitteful, for you not sending us back to prison, but we are ard werkus and willing to learn. Back um, we learnd to count up to XXX, and read the bible, but we em bostin at climbing trees and garding walls, and even learnt to swim."

Cormac turned to his father and murmured, "Perhaps Captain Huw and his crew will train them as seamen ready for our first trading voyage. I have a feeling they will be forever loyal if they learn a useful trade."

The three friends overheard some of the conversation and looked wide-eyed and amazed at the thought of being sailors, so when Cormac turned back to them and said, "We think you might be useful to the Gunnarson family if we had you trained to work on a ship."

Ron said, "Speaking for my companions my lord, we will follow you to the ends of the world and the seven seas."

Ship Shape

"No time like the present," said Cormac. "Thank you for that expression of fealty Ron Rose, and do your companions feel the same?"

"Aye, sir," was the reply.

"For now, just following me to the quayside and will suffice. I will acquaint Captain Preselli with his newest, somewhat less than able seamen."

The trio trooped behind Sir Skeggi and Esquire Cormac down to the riverside to be greeted by the ship's mate Sampson of Gwynedd. "Come aboard the *Merlin* my Lords, are you here to see Captain Huw? He has taken our small boat and is checking on provisions and collecting some spare sails."

Sir Skeggi led the trio up the gangplank that swayed with the ebbing tide, and the lads clung to each other's arms, not wanting to fall into the river as their claim to be good swimmers had been optimistic.

Ship's mate Sampson was well named as he had a chest like a barrel, and taller than anyone they had ever seen, so he towered above the three lads and had a powerful voice, they noticed patterns on his bare arms and Vern whispered to his friends, "I urd that them pictures are called tatt whoos."

Sampson bellowed at them, "Don't you mangy excuses for landlubbers speak unless you are spoken to, and when I say jump to it, you had better be real quick, or you will feel the lash of my knotted rope."

Peter's legs felt like they were turning to calves' foot jelly, and Vernon turned a little pale, while Ron was oblivious, gazing at the masts and furled sails in wonder.

He turned to Cormac and said, "It's a pleasure to see you grown tall and andsome young Sir, and I am proud to meet your famous Viking navigator father. Our captain speaks most highly of you and was most pleased how quickly you gained your sea legs on that trading voyage from Ireland to Fortress Deva.

"As to myself, I have joined Captain Preselli's ship these twelve moons ago, after sailing with his brother's ship, the *Minerva* trading with the lords of Brittany and Kings of Cornwall." Preselli is a surname.

Sir Skeggi and his son each grasped the wrist of the mate in greeting and walked with him to aft of the vessel. "First mate Sampson, my Son and I have had good reports of your sailing skills, but don't be too hard on these three lads. It was our wish that they learn the ways of the sea, and your Captain has instructions to hold you responsible if they are injured."

The mate responded, "Aye, Aye My Lords, but our crew can show them no favours, landlubbers aboard ship can be a liability to everyone's safety."

Sir Skeggi returned to the trio and said, "You will spend the night aboard this ship while it is at anchor, and Mate Sampson will show you where to sleep. But first you will help the crew swab the deck clean and learn how to coil ropes. We will return in the morrow and see how you climb the rigging."

As they left the ship and walked along the quay, Cormac said to his father, "We will have to keep an eye on this Mate Sampson."

LADY VIOLET AND ADOLPHUS

Sir Skeggi, his son Cormac and his daughter in law Grainne met briefly to discuss and decide what needed to be told to Earl Brocmale and his wife Hilda, about the betrothal of Lady Violet to Adolphus?

Grainne said, "This is a delicate matter that will be a shock to my friend Violet and be a discreet warning to her parents, given what you have told us about that scoundrel Adolphus and his being expelled from Wroxeter Abbey School."

Cormac responded, "It is for the best, and my father will ask for a private meeting with Earl Brocmale and his wife, and he in turn will send for confirmation to the Abbott of Wroxeter, before he acts. I will wait outside and join them if invited and inform them of Adolphus' unsuitability as a husband for Violet. Grainne can also be nearby, should Violet need the comfort of a friend."

Much later having returned home to Lady Moya, they told her the news that the betrothal had been annulled, and that Adolphus had been very angry, and intemperate harsh words were spoken, such that he was escorted from the town by the guards, and a poster issued, banning from entering Chester on pain of arrest.

The City guilds were informed and any monies that were owed to them would be claimed by bailiffs, so Adolphus was ruined! He knows nothing of Cormac's involvement, so we can rest assured there will be no retaliation. Lady Grainne would go and offer consolation to Lady Violet in a few days' time.

These distractions were delaying decisions about the first voyage of NEW DEVA TRADING COMPANY, the tithes and gifts for The Pope were now in guarded strongboxes held in a locked crypt of the Church of St John ready to be loaded, shipwrights' plans for a new vessel were agreed and the cost approved and completed by the Company officers. Cormac and his father now needed to board the *Merlin* with Brother Galen and sail with Captain Huw to the mouth of the river Dee to assess the practical matters of wind, tide and navigation and experience the open sea, as Sir Skeggi had only sailed in Viking longboats, before. Then if all were to their satisfaction, the route to Brittany would be agreed, confirming which safe ports to obtain fresh water and food supplies. As sleeping berths were limited, it was agreed that no wives should accompany them, while Cormac wondered if he had made a mistake in allowing the three clumsy Bereminghame lads aboard this ship.

He had heard from captain Huw that the crew had adopted them as amusing mascots and even taught them to play games of draughts, but a simple game of chess was beyond them. Their climbing skills won some grudging approval but that was not under sail, so testing times ahead.

High tide on the River Dee was when Brother Galen, Cormac and Sir Skeggi joined the captain and crew to follow the river down to the sea and waved to a few small fishing boats casting their nets for salmon, the banks of the river were higher than upstream, partly due to earlier efforts of the Roman Legion to improve navigability and stop the silt building as sandbanks. Much of the ship's storage was taken up with two large iron bound chests, filled with heavy stones to be of similar weight to the real cargo to be delivered to Brittany.

The journey to the sea was familiar to Captain Huw who was used to navigating this tidal estuary, but now he was content to point out to the Gunnarsons some of the few landmarks on this otherwise unremarkable route.

"In the distance we can see the place of the holy well of St Winefride. The villagers say it arose by miracle when Winefride's head was chopped off and a spring welled forth. Its water has healing power and is now beginning to be a place of pilgrimage.

"Up on the mountain of Halkyn, lead ore has been mined since the time of the Romans and we have bought the ore as ballast some years gone by. When we are close to the sea the river is wide and has mud banks to avoid, but there is a hermit's island called Hilbre that monks of Chester say was inhabited by St Hildeburgh."

Huw's hand rested on Cormac's shoulder and remarked, "We have no time to visit your friends in Walls Eye or see what changes have been made to Cormac's landing that was once that pirate slaver's lair those four years ago. Maybe another time, for you are their hero and they would feast your return."

As they entered the open sea, the wind began to freshen and the size of the waves increased, Sir Skeggi conferred with captain Huw and they beckoned Cormac to join them, for his eyes were on young Vern, Ron and Peter, the sorry trio of landlubbers. They were arguing whose turn it was to climb the rigging, and Vern began the climb, while the ship rocked in the swell, nimbly reaching the lookout post of the crow's nest. Ron shouted up to him, "See any crows yet?" He heard Vern laughing because a seagull had deposited birdlime on Ron's back.

Peter joined in the merriment and stepped back, only to trip over some coiled rope and fall on his arse. Nearby crew was seen pointing and laughing too, but all were quickly silence by a bellow from Mate Sampson. Before Samson's swift and painful discipline could be practised, Captain Huw intervened and ordered him, "Cut these lads some slack, Mister Samson." And only Cormac noticed the mate scowl and mutter some obscene oath.

Cormac now joined his father and the Captain and for the next period of the ships watch, he was instructed on the use of the sunstone, a crystal of Iceland spar needed when the sun was hidden by clouds. "This is my first gift to you, on future voyages, always wear my sunstone around your neck using this thong."

"Next, here is my lodestone the needles show the direction of North and South, you partly fill this bowl with water and the needle floating inside a straw points the way, keep it safe," said his father gravely. "The lives of your crew and the ship may depend up it."

Captain Huw remarked, "What your father said is true, and these are gifts without price. Our voyage together to Brittany may depend upon it."

Raven's Return

Back at Ecclestone Manor, Grainne had sent a servant for some sweet cakes of honey, nuts and raisins and a pitcher of the first season's wine from Portmore Manor vineyards. They had become favourites of her father Earl Edwin who liked to pore over some of his son-in-law's maps in the afternoon sunshine, and she found him seated in the small arbour where she was told her late mother often sat. The place was fragrant with honeysuckle and all was quiet save for the murmur of bees returning to the hives.

She sat beside him and thanked the servant for the small repast, then poured some wine for both of them and asked, "Dear father, don't you ever wish for a female companion to share this life? It has been over 15 years since mother died."

The Earl looked at his lovely daughter and sighed a little because Grainne looked so much like her mother, who would have delighted to see her grown into a woman, but death in childbirth had claimed her. "I have been content to watch you grow and blossom, and I delight in seeing you happily married to Cormac. But yes, maybe a companion chatelaine would ease the lonely hours when you are away from me."

His daughter smiled and grew thoughtful and laughingly replied, "Perhaps a voyage on The Merlin to Brittany would find you a demure princess."

Edwin responded a little more cheerfully, "Well you were never demure, young lady; more of shield maiden was your style."

She got up, and nibbling on a sweet cake, wandered off to be alone with her thoughts discovering that she would miss her husband when he would soon be away on his first trading voyage. Walking to the manor watchtower by the river, she stopped some way off and felt a rush of wind at her shoulder. Then something gripped the top of her head and she heard that eerie sound **'hrokar, hrokar'** that Cormac had described as Odin's messenger raven.

The large bird with magnificent black plumage and an almost golden beak had come to her, not her husband, and it now hopped onto her outstretched arm. She was amazed and not a little afraid. "Greetings mistress, now I am also your messenger enabling you to reach your husband whenever he carries the tarn helm. When you married Cormac, you became one and I am ready to serve you, just like I did when Skeggi and his son were sailing to meet each other these four years past. I am only visible to you and the Gunnarson family."

This is indeed a blessing of the Old Gods, and God works with many folk and creatures that are part of His plans, she mused quietly. "So, Odin's crow, do you have a name?"

The wily bird hopped onto her other arm and croaked his reply, "Odin always called me crow, so that will suffice. You cannot speak my real name for it is in Corvus speech."

Grainne nodded appearing to seem wise, but answered simply, "Crow it shall be then. This is my message to him, as I am curious to see if you can find him. Simply say 'My palm is itching to be scratched again', he alone will know that it is me speaking through you, Crow."

Meanwhile, aboard the *Merlin*, Cormac idly watched the Mate at the ship's rudder and Captain Huw who was relaying orders to the crew to reduce sail as the ship manoeuvred in the big circle that would head them back to the River Dee, making adjustments for currents, and cross winds.

One of the crew said to Cormac, "Good Sir, in the distance you may see the Isle of Ynys Mon, once the land of Druids, and sailing through the narrow Straits of Menai has seen many a shipwreck."

The sailor moved away, and Brother Galen made his way over to Cormac, holding tight to low rigging as the deck heeled over. There came a cry of, "Ship approaching!" Almost all turned their heads to look, but it was only fishermen returning with their catch of crabs.

Galen held onto Cormac to steady himself and asked, "When we sail for Brittany may we visit Aleth in Armorica and the mount of Saint Malo? He came from our monastery of Llancarfan Abbey in my land of Wales, and we are told he sailed with Brendan the Navigator, hundreds of years gone by."

Cormac frowned a little trying to recall the scroll and maps he had brought from Wroxeter Abbey, when Odin's raven perched on his wrist and the tarn helm slung at his belt quivered. Momentarily startled, he heard the once familiar croak of '**hrokar, hrokar**', and then Galen looked at him in astonishment saying, "There is a crow on your wrist!"

Now it was Cormac's turn to be alarmed, and looking around him, he saw none of the crew were taking any notice, and sighed with relief saying, "This is a holy messenger bird, but has always been invisible to others except father and myself."

Brother Galen made a hasty sign of the cross and said, "Thank the saints I am not seeing a demon, but recently my dreams have been filled with talking birds. I am a brother of the Franciscan Order, and St Francis talked to creatures."

The raven spoke to Cormac, but Galen heard nothing except croaking noises, the raven uttered, "This is my first message, 'My palm is itching to be scratched again'. It comes from someone close to your heart, but many leagues distant."

Cormac blushed and replied, say, "My Love, our ship is already heading back and will soon reach the Dee estuary. I will be home in a few hours."

The raven flew off and he turned to Brother Galen and speaking gravely and in undertones he answered, "I beg you consider this news to be as if it was in your confessional, and to be spoken of with no-one except my family."

Swiftly his answer came, "By all that is sacred, this is a miraculous occurrence, a gift from the Holy Trinity, and will remain sacrosanct, but I am eager to know more!"

Cormac pondered how much to reveal to this man of God and decided to be less than honest on what might cause a severe test of faith for his friend. "The raven is an unexpected wonder that is connected with my holy cards blessed by the hermit of Skellig. Many creatures feature in what I call, *Brother Kell's Book of Spells*. The raven card has enabled me to send and receive messages, but only from father to son and son to father. Now since the blessing of my marriage to Grainne we are now One under God and, now she too can send and receive messages."

Tons of Drinks

Lady Moya now had a wet nurse to look after baby Julia and had more time to oversee processing the apples and grapes at Portmore Manor. The harvest had been plentiful, and she wanted to expand the production of cider and wines, so over a meal with her husband Skeggi, her son Cormac and her daughter in law Grainne she raised the matter of needing to employ a carpenter and blacksmith to make larger barrels for fermentation, and more smaller ones to store the finished product while ageing.

Local churches and monasteries had already placed orders for sacramental wine, and a few of the taverns no longer wished to operate their own brew houses as the customers preferred Portmore Cider.

The others applauded her success and Grainne remarked, "Having our own smithy and carpenter, with apprentices and making a deal with the Vintners Guild would mean more hands to work on building more of your chariots."

Cormac kissed his wife and raised his cup in a toast, "To Gunnarson Family Enterprises and prosperity."

Plans and ideas for provisioning and cargoes for the next voyage of the Merlin kept the family talking for hours until Cormac yawned and stood up holding his wife's hand and said, "Time for bed, my love."

She giggled and replied, "I have been expecting you to say that for some time now, but you are so full of ideas. But now I have some of my own. We bid you goodnight."

A month later, after mass in St John's church, The Abbot Peter and his treasurer invited the Gunnarson family to join them in his Vestry and informed them that two iron-bound and locked chests were now sealed and ready to be transported to Brittany. This would be the first part of their long journey to The Pope in Rome, and four armed soldiers would be aboard ship to guard the gold and silver, keeping watch, in turns day and night.

The Abbot prayed a prayer of blessing and safety on the special cargo and the ship's crew. He handed a sealed scroll to Cormac to hand over when he reached St Malo, and expected another sealed scroll noting the exchange and handover of responsibility to the latest successor of the first Abbot – Aaron of Aletum.

It was time to visit the Merlin recently docked from a short voyage and see Captain Huw about special storage for the holy cargo, but then he would need to return home to supervise the dismantling of 3 new chariots, one of them a specially commissioned gift to The Pope, decked in royal purple seats, and stained purple leather harness. The wheels had been edged with their blacksmith's iron; the same bands used for the wine barrels.

Cormac's wife and parents now left for home and he walked down to the Water Gate docks, and was welcomed aboard, but Mate Sampson was nowhere to be seen. His latest act of brutality on the youngest of the crew had not gone unnoticed and he was discharged from duty and left behind in a northern port.

BEST MATE

Pleased and mildly curious that Captain Huw had hired another mate to serve on the *Merlin*, Cormac followed him aft and was delighted and surprised to see the new man was none other than his father's step brother, the Viking Rognvald who he had freed from slavery more than four years ago!

"Uncle!" he called out.

Rognvald cried out, "By Thor's mighty hammer, how tall you have grown! Is this young Cormac of the killer basilisk egg, saver of young maidens and destroyer of pirate lairs? My Captain hired me because we are related and admired my skill at the oars."

Cormac found himself wrapped in a bear hug and lifted off his feet and swung around, to the amusement of the nearby crew, who looked at Cormac with new respect. Cormac gasped and got enough breath back to share some back slapping and enquired, "You old rascal, did you persuade the captain to keep your presence a secret? This is a great surprise and an even bigger one for my family when you are re-united with them. We have so much to tell you, and you will have tales of serving Earl Thorkel."

Turning to Captain Huw he asked, "May I have your permission to allow Mate Rognvald sometime ashore to dine with my family? You, of course, are invited too."

Returning to Portmore Manor with Rognvald, Cormac had time to tell him of the many changes since they had parted those four years ago and agreed Rognvald's story would wait until he had greeted Skeggi, Moya and Grainne. Captain Huw's duties meant he would visit them a little later.

Cormac ran ahead to alert his family of Skeggi's half-brother's return, and they all walked out to meet him, including Earl Edwin who was visiting his daughter. The two reunited Vikings held each other in a fierce embrace and tears streamed down Rognvald's cheeks as he went on to hug Moya and Grainne and hold baby Julia high on his shoulders to her evident delight.

Earl Edwin came forward to shake Rognvald's hand and said with a voice thick with emotion, "You saved me from those pirate slavers in Liuerpul and returned me to my health and family; I shall be eternally in your debt."

Rognvald looked around in wonder at the size and grandness of the manor (Rognvald had been on a slave ship, never visited manor?)and remarked, "I have seen nothing like this in my voyages from Orkney to the land of the Franks, although the country of The Visigoths has some fine estates, the God's have blessed you my brother."

Moya replied, "All our family are now baptised Christians, so it is the One true God we worship and serve here and His blessings we enjoy."

Supper was a celebration feast, a time of much joy, amusement and gasps as each member of the family had tales to tell of the last four years, and Rognvald could see what he had missed while apart from this loving and prosperous family, so spoke of the chiefs he had met, the sometimes strange customs of other islands and lands, and the foods and drinks he had been offered and enjoyed. He discretely did not mention the encounters with many women, but told them he had not yet married, but took the opportunity to drink a toast to Cormac and Grainne and expressed a desire to ride in a chariot sometime.

Sailor Tales

The women began to yawn and sigh after the evening sky showed a full moon and the bright evening star, for they rose from bed earlier than their men, so they both said goodnight to the men who had now begun to broach a new cask of wine.

Huw and Rognvald shared tales of the ports they had known and the venal customs officials eager to extract a larger fee or bribe, to overlook certain cargoes and damages from the dockside tavern brawls. Sir Skeggi realised that having left the Viking life behind, where fear and death came with longboats on the horizon, trading required a different skill. Cormac wanted to know more of the local chiefs, Kings and Dukes and what gifts he might need to offer to have trading concession granted, also letters of safe conduct?

He was advised that Alliances were known to shift between kingdoms and wars were often a hindrance to trade and the safety of ships was at risk from being commandeered. During these times, spies were everywhere and trade in weapons was dangerous and risky. Employing local guides and translators was necessary, but it was wise to not disclose to strangers that you understood their local language.

Cormac listened intently and earlier had refused further wine, to keep a clear head and absorb as much knowledge of sailing and trade matters as he could, thinking, "Brother Kell's cards will be much in demand on my first voyage, as will Odin's raven and careful use of the tarn helm."

Captain Huw mentioned dealings with the Franks whose leaders and officials spoke Latin, but local traders often used confusing versions known as Frankreich, Franrijk and Frankrig, but also Saxon and some Friesian. That is when you needed to recruit some extra local sailors to explain local customs.

Ever curious, Cormac wanted to know a little of the Visigoths who had once invaded Rome and now ruled the lands south of the Franks that the Romans called Iberia. Brother Galen had advised him that these southern lands also included the Northern coasts of the Western middle sea.

Neither Huw nor Rognvald had ever ventured to that land, but there were tales of hot sunshine under blue skies and colourful fruits, some that tasted sweet and other yellow ones tasted sour. The juices of both fruits provided delicious drinks with healing properties, and olive trees were cultivated since Roman time and their fruits were crushed to provide a liquid to replace animal fats when cooking.

At this revelation, there was a thoughtful silence, and more wine was shared, but the men were already thinking of the profits if these fruits could be shipped home without becoming spoiled? Maybe these fruits and others might be found along the shores of the lands of the Middle sea and knowledge gained as to what they might be traded for and even transported successfully? Could these marvellous trees be brought home and new orchards planted? All present agreed that they should sleep on these matters, and despite an offer of a bed, Captain and his Mate needed to be back aboard the. Merlin

In the Cards Again

The next morning, Cormac woke early his mind buzzing with plans for the voyage to Brittany and reached into the hidden pocket in his old cloak, to see what inspiration Brother Kell's cards might offer.

His young wife was a light sleeper, and she awoke too, and asked if aught was amiss? "I have the holy cards before me, and I ponder which of them I will be led to use?"

Yawning a little she replied, "After I left you last night, seeking our bed, what emerged as your most needful asset from the talks with your trading partners?"

He responded, "Captain Huw has not yet been told of the holy magic in these cards, nor of the raven messenger or the tarn helm. The fewer folk that know outside our family, the better. Perhaps you might help me choose the next holy cards I might use, but do tell me why?"

Grainne reached over his body to hold the cards, and as she did so, a tingle ran through her fingers and up her arm, which startled her, and the cards spilled onto their bed sheet. A faint glow emanated from the picture of a large bird and she exclaimed, "Cormac, the card before us I recognise as an Albatross? This is a sign of wonder as I dreamt of a large bird last night just like this. This creature can soar high into the sky and you will be enabled to see what lies ahead or behind the ship, much sooner than the lookout in the crow's nest?"

Cormac gazed adoringly at his wife, 'Holy Mother of God, by all the saints; you are now blessed by Brother Kell, too! In Brittany I will not reveal my grasp of languages that comes from the holy card of St Peter, and thus discern if translators are honest, and be silently aware of their talk with others. An excellent advantage when bargaining with traders and Chiefs." They gazed into each other's eyes, and both became flushed with desire, so they were quite late coming for breakfast.

When Moya and her daughter had spoken to the cook about the evening meal, they walked out to the orchard and vineyards to check on the latest batch of cider, and the wine press, and then had time to collect baby Julia, who was now crawling and set her on a blanket on an area of grass. Meanwhile Cormac came to inspect the smithy, and found the three lads, Peter, Vern & Ron polishing and staining the wood of parts of the chariots.

They stood to attention and attempted a salute and Ron touched his forelock and spoke, "Us lads is right chuffed to be learnin' a new traide yer honour, and before you is the last of them three chariots, we 'ave assemberulled."

Cormac beamed at the progress his protégés had made, and asked, "Your endeavours should be rewarded, would you like to take turns and ride my own chariot with me?"

They looked at him open mouthed and in unison replied, "That am reelly bostin yer honour."

So, to the amusement, and not a little envy, some of the farm workers and kitchen staff gathered to watch, as each lad took his turn to ride up and down the path to the manor's landing stage.

Peter was last and, on his return, had turned a little pale and almost fell off the chariot crying, "Weem flew faster than the wind!"

CHARTING A COURSE

Sir Skeggi and his son Cormac had been aboard the *Merlin* for a while since noon and after bread, cheese and wine, Captain Huw spread out before them his maps and charts that enabled him to plot a course for Brittany. Father and Son had never travelled the sea lanes that traversed the Welsh Kingdoms that began with Gwynedd in the north, south east along Ceredigion, then west and south around Dyfed, the Gwyr, and then east to Morgannwg.

They would avoid Gwent that took them into the channel formed by the estuary of River Severn. He advised negotiating for fresh water and food would best be served by him, as he had visited these bays and inlets many times and welcomed due to his family estate in Gwynedd and being related to the descendant of Cadfan ap Iago.

Huw explained that Local Chiefs and Kings required some tribute, but monasteries and churches welcomed all who came in peace and Cormac's connections with Skellig, the Abbess Cecelia of Bees

Head and Brother Tudno, also his knowledge of Latin would enhance their welcome. But first they must navigate the narrow strait of Menai, rather than go around the isle of Mona to the open sea and encounter pirates.

Huw explained that after leaving the coast of Gwynedd they would traverse the wide bay of Ceredigion where he was less well known. An early leader of that realm was Cunedda who had migrated there from the South West land of the Scots, and near the southern port of Abergwaun bards sing of the holy man Carranog who had a magic floating altar!

Sir Skeggi shook his head wonderingly and remarked, "Strange are the ways and legends of the Welsh."

His son replied, "No more so than tales of the Norse Gods."

Our Welsh kingdoms are full of the deeds of new holy men who have been made Saints in the time of my grandfather's memories, you Saxons will come to revere the names of Dewi who you know as David and the monastery of St Non his father, and Patrick famous throughout Hibernia, advisor to Kings of Ireland.

At this, Cormac nodded, remembering stories of St Patrick, told by the monk in his village of Portmore, and remarked, "It will be a great adventure to sail with you once more Captain, but my companions and guards will struggle to sleep in your hammocks. May we see where you will store the Abbott's strong boxes, and the parts of my two chariots, one intended for the Holy Father in Rome?"

Satisfied with the storage area, Cormac told Huw that Abbott Peter would be coming to bless the voyage, and offer a prayer, and bring letters of introduction and safe conduct to be shown to all who would hinder their journey, under threat of excommunication. The Abbot would explain their voyage as a pilgrimage to holy places in Brittany.

'Farewell and bon voyage'

Skeggi promised Moya most faithfully, that this would be his last voyage. He was mindful of the need to train their son in the arts of navigation on the open seas and intended to bequeath his precious Viking instruments to Cormac, who hoped to have his own ship, one day. Skeggi rashly promised to return with gifts, special ones for Moya and baby Julia.

Earl Edwin and Grainne said their separate farewells to Cormac and offered prayers of, "God Speed the *Merlin*, and all who sailed on her." While Brother Galen and his monks held a special Mass led by Abbott Peter, and attended by Brocmale, The Earl of Chester, his family, and leaders of the Guilds of Chester, some secretly anxious about their investment in NEW DEVA TRADING COMPANY.

The Abbott blessed the gifts being sent to the Pope via Brittany. The somewhat godless crew and Mate Rognvald had spent their last night in the taverns and brothels, and some lit a candle in the church, just in case.

Captain Huw had spent the previous night aboard his ship, seeing to the armed guards and their special cargo, and setting a watch on the dock area, gangplank raised. He looked forward to their first port of call, Caernafon in Gwynedd, and the familiar view of the ruins of fortress Segontium, but most of all spending the night with his wife Elwys and son Aaron in nearby Caethro. His wife claimed her bloodline reached back to the Ordovice tribe.

His own practical prayer was that there would be no deserters among the crew this time, unlikely given the less than welcoming nature of ports in the west and south of Wales, who were suspicious of foreigners, having long memories of Roman attacks in years gone by.

Wanting to make his first trading voyage to be memorable and make the departure have a sense of occasion to the townsfolk, Cormac had hired some of the musicians who had performed at his wedding to play some cheerful ,but well know sea songs and some sacred music. He was gratified when the onlookers, wives and sweethearts shouted and applauded. He even provided free cups of Portmore cider, much to the delight of the poorer folk.

Finally, in full regalia, the Abbott and his choir boys, one carrying the large cross, came in procession to the landing stage and calling for silence he prayed, "Ebb tide, full tide, praise the Lord of land and sea, barren rocks, darting birds, praise His holy name. Poor folk, ruling folk, praise the Lord of land and sea. Noble women, chanting priests, slaves set free, praise his holy name. AMEN."

So, at last the anchor was raised and stored, the ropes and hawsers taken aboard, and taking advantage of the high tide, the ship began its journey to the open sea. It carried the hopes, dreams, and fears of those left behind, but the thrill of adventure swelled the hearts of Skeggi, Rognvald and Cormac, new lands and new challenges lay ahead.

Family Visit

Reaching the open sea once more, extra sail was hoisted and they headed west along the coast of Gwynedd, not stopping this time at The Great Orme, but saw that the hermit Tudnohad now built a small church instead of the cave where Cormac had met him four years ago, a man in a cassock wave to them, and he recalled with a shiver the prophecy about a future Saxon leader and some burnt cakes.

Soon they would drop the anchor and rest until daybreak., so Brother Galen obtained the captain's permission to lead a small act of worship that included a bible passage and short prayers.

Afterwards, some of the crew thanked him and asked for confession and absolution. While Cormac remembered the ancient prayer, his mother offered it when they were leaving, "May the raindrops fall lightly on your brow, may the soft winds freshen your spirit. May the sunshine brighten your heart. May the burdens of the day rest lightly upon you and may God enfold you in love."

When he had passed by the river Conwy, the captain pointed to the large island of Ynys Mon on the horizon, once the lair of Druids who were slaughtered by Romans, destroying their sacred groves of oak, shrines, and menhirs. Irish Kings and pirates later conquered and settled, they in turn were defeated by Cadwallon Lawhir , (which meant long hand), and stories tell that he could reach a stone from the ground to kill a raven, without bending his back, because his arm was as long as his side to the ground! Cormac exclaimed, "Of course my grandfather Bedwyr loved to tell me stories of King

Bran the Blessed of Gwynedd and many other tales in the Mabinogi."

Tides and currents were dangerous when passing through Menai and all who were not crew were invited to take hold of rigging for their safety, this passage was known for shipwrecks, but it seemed the fervent prayers of the Gunnarson women and the Abbott saved them from harm. Despite the howling winds and some bouts of lashing rain, they saw a welcoming beacon on the highest point of the ruins of Fortress Segontium, the captain was smiling and told his crew and passengers, "That is my home town, here we anchor for a night and bring on fresh water and fresh meats and vegetables, sadly not yet the season for our juicy plums."

The crews' eyes gleamed in anticipation of savouring the delights of their favourite tavern and the boisterous greeting that awaited them from the serving wenches, Mate Rognvald duties meant he had to stay aboard with the guards, while Huw invited Skeggi and Cormac to meet his family in nearby Caethro.

The setting sun cast its gleam on the sea turning it to look like liquid gold, and Cormac summoned Odin's raven and told him to stand watch unseen, looking out for anyone attempting to board the *Merlin*, and in his mind for the first time he seemed to hear a reply from the bird, complaining he was Odin's messenger, not a lookout, and Cormac frowned a little thinking, *does this bird know my thoughts?*

TESSERAE

With Captain Huw leading the way, Sir Skeggi, his son and brother Galen took the well beaten track to meet the captain's family, and Cormac carried a gift of small, sealed amphora of Portmore Manor cider and red wine. Young Aaron ran down the garden path to meet his father who lifted him up on his broad shoulders, and laughing said, "How you've grown young rascal."

Huw's wife Elwys stood at the door of their home wearing a simple but becoming gown of an unusual cloth and greeted them, "Croeso i gymru' she said in the Welsh tongue, and Cormac quickly replied 'Diolch yn fawr ichi Boneddiges."

She continued, "As a captain's wife he has taught me many useful phrases in other languages, and my son is learning your Saxon tongue.' Noticing the monk, she bowed and made the sign of the cross and he in turn said, "Domina mea, ut benedicat tibi bona."

Huw took his wife in his arms and kissed her soundly saying, "It is so good to be homefy nghariad (my darling), these three men are my good friends, and we are on a trading mission to Brittany, which God willing will improve all our fortunes and our voyage has been blessed by the Bishop of Chester, and aboard ship, we carry a gift for The Pope."

As they stepped over the threshold Brother Galen hesitated and cried out, "We must take off our shoes. "The others looked down and gasped in amazement, for the floor was covered, not in packed earth and fresh dried rushes, but in an intricate many coloured mosaic depicting birds and flowers!

Galen turned to the others and said, "This is indeed a wonder, for I have seen floors such as this in Roman palaces and churches."

Husband and wife stood proud, and he said, "I bought this plot of land many years ago and when my brother helped me dig out some foundations, we discovered this treasure."

Cormac exclaimed, "Those tiny tiles are called Tesserae, made from fired earths, polished pebbles and coloured glasses."

Elwys invited them in and insisted they stay for a meal, for which they thanked her most warmly. She set before them *picws mali* which she explained was crushed oat bread in buttermilk, this was followed by *Cawl a* stew made with lamb, leeks and root vegetables, and the juices that remained were mopped up with lava bread. "It's made from a special seaweed, cooked and coated in oats," she told them.

Brother Galen replied, "It has the flavour of the sea and goes so well with the Cawl."

Cormac thought to himself, "As a child I disliked oats, but I delight in their usefulness, now."

Elwys blushed at the compliments, and gladly tasted both the wine and then the cider and offering a little of that to young Aaron murmured, "Your Portmore wine and cider is as fine as any my husband has brought me back from his voyages."

Song for Harp

Huw called his son over and said, "Bring the harp my lad; I know you have been practising, then go and sit by your mother. I understand you will soon play at our Noson Lawen."

"Shall I play 'The March of the White Monks of Bangor, father?'" he enquired.

Hearing this, Brother Galen stood up and asked, "May I sing along to this song of Christian martyrs?"

Elwys also stood and replied, "It would be an honour if you sang it with me." So, the rippling tones of the harp filled the room, and the duet began, and soon the listeners were enthralled by the beauty and clarity of the two voices. Then the tempo increased, and feet started to tap, and Elwys hips began to sway in time until finally the song ended, and the family hound howled mournfully.

Galen clapped his hands in sheer delight, and remarked, "Such a change from plainsong at Matins, and you played your harp really well, Bless you my Son."

The evening had passed swiftly and reluctantly Cormac said to his father." We must bid this family good night, for now we need to return to the *Merlin*."

Elwys handed a small platter of the *picws mali* and a bowl of *Cawl* saying, "Please take this back to the ship for the Mate, after all he is your kin, Sir Skeggi."

On the way back to the harbour Brother Galen took a small phial held on a thread around his neck and showed it proudly to Cormac, saying, "Many years ago I trained as a priest at The Holy Isle of Lindisfarne, and the Abbott gave me this as a parting gift, saying it was a holy oil from the time of Saint Aidan. Recently I have been given visions of your ship in peril from high waves and storm, and the message God will Provide."

Back on board the *Merlin*, Rognvald gratefully accepted Elwy's gift and begged permission to have an evening ashore with two of the special cargo guards, promising they would return before dawn. Odin's raven appeared before Cormac and his father with the familiar 'hrokar, hrokar' greeting and in his mind, Cormac heard the message, "No new human has nested in this floating tree," and promptly vanished.

He turned to Skeggi and said, "Our pet raven has been on guard, and our cargo is safe."

His father replied, "Your crow is better than Earl Thorkel's wolf hounds, Fenris and Loki, they would have just howled." Cormac was a little surprised; he had never heard any tales of the Viking life his father had led in the ten years he spent away from Moya and Grandfather Bedwyr. So, they conversed quietly together, after checking on the other two guards and providing them with an amphora of cider and agreeing to stand guard in their place for the next ship's watch.

Skeggi revealed a little about his sea voyages to Shetland and Gotland while serving his Earl, and the navigation skills he had learned, becoming so useful, that despite asking to return to Portmore and his family, his requests fell on deaf ears. It was only when Earl Thorkel acquired a younger second wife and became besotted and no longer wished to go a-viking. Finally, Skeggi was granted a last voyage to Chester, and so mother and son finally were reunited with him. The Gunnarson family had ten years apart, and now we have had four years together and God willing many more ahead.

Holy Cards

Cormac responded to the story of his father's earlier life serving Earl Thorkel by taking out the cards of Brother Kell's Holy spells (or more correctly invocations) and showed him their variety and splendour.

He said, "I am still learning to be cautious in their use, but have found they seem to be capable of being used more than once; so far the Basilisk card has had the most destructive power, for it enabled me to destroy the lair of the evil pirate slavers of Liuerpul, and rescue Grainne's father'. Just as the raven of Odin helped us become finally reunited, so the high-flying bird cards have shown me what dangers may lie miles away."

Skeggi nodded thoughtfully saying, "We have much to thank your ancestor and the hermit of Skellig, for they have brought you a beautiful young wife and Portmore Manor, and your mother and me the blessing of baby Julia."

Dawn was now breaking, and a watery sun was appearing over the horizon, when Brother Galen returned aboard followed by the last of the crew and guards, and next Captain Huw carrying a jug, who waved farewell to his wife Moya on the quayside-their son Aaron was still abed.

Finally, Mate Rognvald arrived with two tavern wenches, one on each arm. He kissed them soundly and they begged him to return again soon. The captain gave the order to muster the crew, raise anchor and draw in the mooring ropes, for it would soon be high tide declaring, "We plot a course for Ceredigion and the bay of Cardigan."

Once more Brother Galen led the crew in prayer, raising his right hand and calling upon God the Father to give them fair winds and calm seas while holding the phial of holy oil in his left hand....

Skeggi and his son told the Captain that they would try and sleep for a few hours, but to wake them earlier if needed, so they were gently woken by Rognvald before midday and offered a drink of warm goat's milk that Moya had thoughtfully provided. The rich taste brought back memories for Cormac of his childhood in Portmore, and he delighted in the change from cow's milk sold in Chester.

Brother Galen invited them to walk to the ship's prow and showed them Bardsey Island he remarked,

"Also known as Ynys Enlli." With small a huddle of buildings and its distinctive St Mary's abbey it was where he has spent the summer as a novice. The island community was dependent upon visits by local fisherman as wild seas meant the community was cut off for many days.

Sadly, they had no time to pay the monks a visit, so he blessed them from a distance. The area of land they had skirted was known as Llyn, and there were ancient tales of the earth quaking in that region. The weather changed and dark clouds from the west soon brought heavy rain, so Captain Huw brought four sealskin capes that would deflect most of the downpour, but the sounds of thunder began to roll, and lightning flashed in the skies, and they saw the top rigging blazing in a blue-ish violet glow and Galen cried out, "We call this "Candles of the Holy Ghost", there is no heat, but do not touch!"

EXCHANGE OF NEWS

Only Cormac and Brother Galen stood staring in wonder at the sight of violet fire that did not burn the rigging, for the crew and Skeggi were used to this sight and the priest exclaimed, "Now I know a little of what Moses felt when he saw the burning bush."

Skeggi joined them saying, "That violet fire is nothing compared to the skies in the far North where the heavens display swirling colours. Shamans tell us it was revealing the Bifrost bridge."

Now they saw the storm abate, and the skies clear and the trio heard the flutter of wings and the croaking of Odin's raven, causing Brother Galen to make the sign of the cross. Then the bird rested on Cormac's arm and in his head, he heard the raven ask, "Do you have a message for your family?"

He looked across to his father and inquired, "Shall we have Odin's raven tell our family that all is well?"

Skeggi frowned a little but then smiled and replied, "Both our wives will be anxious to know of our progress."

So, without speaking he asked the bird to say to Grainne, "We are sailing round the bay of Cardigan and had met Captain Huw's wife, Elwys and their son living near the old fortress of Segontium- the floor of their home is a wonder. Ask them is all well with Moya and baby Julia, and was Portmore Manor prospering under your supervision?"

Back at Portmore Manor, Moya and her daughter in law Grainne were resting in the late afternoon sunshine and trying to keep baby Julia amused and distract her from teething discomforts, when the child spoke her first word saying, "Bird."

The ladies looked at each other in astonishment, and then in awed understanding as Odin's raven perched on Grainne's shoulder and they heard the familiar croaking 'Hrokar'.

Moya exclaimed, "I hear, but do not see the bird."

Her companion replied, "I see it, but only hear the croaking, a silent message forms in my mind, and it's from your son. He tells me all is well, and they have met Captain Huw's family and are now sailing the bay of Cardigan."

Moya's face expressed relief and she recalled seeing the name of the bay on Cormac route plans, and Grainne nodded agreement.

The baby gurgled and spoke again, "Bird, bird." And reached out to touch the raven, who hopped out of reach onto Grainne's right hand.

Moya arose and picked up her daughter, and said gently, "Are you ready to tell your husband the good news, that your first child will be born before he returns?"

Grainne looked at Moya and answered, "How long have you known? Only in these past few weeks have I realised that my monthly courses had stopped and begun to hope that I was with child."

Cormac's mother smiled and said, "Back in Ireland, I was often called upon to help the midwife who respected my knowledge and skills with herbs, and my own mother claimed I had the Second Sight, but I have revealed that to no-one, as Holy Mother Church does not approve."

Both ladies beamed with happiness, and Grainne said tremulously, "I will send the news with Odin's raven, when I am sure."

MIXED EMOTIONS

Grainne sat alone in her room and considered what message she would send to the father of their child, who although among his friends and living the dream of sailing miles from home on a trading venture, would now carry the extra burden of fatherhood. Would he be pleased but also anxious that he may not now return home in time for the birth?

She began to rehearse in her mind what she might say, and emotions began to well up inside and almost overwhelm her, because for the first time since her childhood she thought of the mother who died giving birth to her, leaving behind a distraught and sometimes distant husband.

She realised that her father had channelled all his love into rearing a daughter who resembled his wife and was a constant reminder of his loss. She offered a prayer of thanks to Mary, Mother of God that she was blessed by her own fruit of the womb, and the solace and comfort of Cormac's mother, Lady Moya who herself had coped with an absent husband.

Another curious thought distracted her, where did Odin's raven go when not conveying messages, could it be linked to the tarn helm, but that was with Cormac on the *Merlin*? Was the Gunnarson family connected by holy webs of wonder fashioned by Norse Gods, but transformed by the Holy Ghost? Was her relationship and pregnancy part of a larger plan from heaven? She decided she would sleep on it for maybe her dreams would afford an answer, and before drifting off in slumber she wondered if their child would be a boy or girl and maybe inherit the fiery red hair of Vikings.

At dawn she was awoken by a need to seek the privy and when she had bathed, the now familiar croak of the raven emanated from her bedroom. Her dreams had revealed nothing, so she stroked the bird's glossy black feathers and said, "Wonderful clever bird, favourite servant of Odin, deliver this message to Cormac- I am so proud of you dear husband I pray for your safety and success every night, also for that of your father, the captain and Brother Galen. But more than the wealth that successful trade might bring I send you my love and that of your mother and baby sister Julia, because in 8 months' time she will have a new baby to play with, for we are to blessed with a child of our own'.

Unexpectedly, the raven circled her room twice and picked up a thin gold bangle inscribed with the letters C & G that had been a wedding gift and flew off.

Joining Moya and the baby to break their fast together, she now began to take a discreet interest on how Julia was fed, and the progress she was making in producing her first teeth, and how Moya soothed her by feeding from her breast, no need for wet nurses in this manor she thought. She realised that no servant was required to change the babe's soiled undergarment, a task that Moya undertook without a qualm.

Fatherhood

Captain Huw advised Cormac and his father that they needed more fresh water and would be heading for Llangranog; at this Brother Galen's face smiled in recognition saying, "During my novice days studying under an old Abbott, he would interrupt our theology discussions, to tell me of Welsh Saint Carantoc. He was a hermit who once lived in the shadow of Carrog Beca, that tall rock you can see above that sandy beach, legends say it was a tooth spat out by the giant Beca. There was a healing well nearby, and its overflow created a waterfall, that's where we fill our water butts."

Mate Rognvald gave the order to change course and they anchored in a small bay, a better option that entering the River Gwaun and its fishing port of Abergwaun surround by steep hills. Cormac had not slept well, anxious for Odin's raven to bring news of home and so was relieved when heard the birds familiar greeting '**hrokar, hrokar**', and walked aft to join Skeggi, so they might both hear the message in private. They both laid hands on the tarn helm attached to Cormac's waist, and their minds were attuned to family news reaching them from afar.

With the news relayed, huge smiles of delight spread across their faces, and only with great effort did either of them refrain from shouting out the momentous news, but instead they grasped each other in a bear hug, with Cormac saying quietly to his father, "Grainne is to have our child, you will be a grandfather, and Earl Edwin will be one, too."

It seemed like a hundred questions were racing through Cormac's mind as his education had not included the understanding of the miracle of birth. He needed to share the news with Brother Galen that they might offer up prayers together for the safety of his wife, which he did, once more explaining it was a holy vision.

For now, the news had to be a secret shared by only a select few and hoped that his father Skeggi would not tell his own half-brother, Mate Rognvald, who could not be trusted, when drunk.

This time the raven rested patiently on the ships rigging, and so Cormac thoughtfully fed the bird with a morsel of salted fish as a reward, which it swallowed eagerly, so our euphoric father-to –be fetched a honeycomb still full of honey and added it to a ladle of fresh water and offered it to the bearer of glad tidings.

He said, "Well done mighty bird, maybe you are descended from the raven that nested in the Ark of Noah." He ruffled the feathers behind the bird's neck and said, "Fly off to a well-earned rest; maybe you are blessed with a mate and chicks?"

Feeling happy and relaxed he gazed in wonder at the porpoises gliding around the ship's bow and saw grey seals basking on the rocks of a small island.

TROUBLED WATERS

Whilst Skeggi wanted to send a message with Odin's raven to his wife Moya, he knew that first, his son needed time alone to gather his tender thoughts and express his feelings to Grainne and talk of what the future will hold for them as parents-to–be. So, calling for the raven to attend him Cormac was relieved to feel the bird settle upon his head and croak the now familiar avian greeting.

His mind was filled with a myriad of thoughts and emotions, but finally he began Wondrous bird, you must tell my wife Grainne that this message is for her alone and say, "My dearest wife, the news you sent that you are having our child fills me with overwhelming joy but also not a little concern that I am not there with you, to embrace you and kiss you and profess my undying love. So, our prayers of thanksgiving to The Trinity must be made separately.

"Please seek the advice of wise women, so you will know what to expect to happen to your sweet body and to our child in your womb, in the months that lie ahead. Please ensure you have regular visits from a Doctor who is trusted by Brother Galen and Lady Hilda, Countess of Chester. I desperately wish there were some way I could return to your side now, but THE NEW DEVA TRADING COMPANY is relying on me to deliver the gifts to the Pope.

"I am sure that you will hear many old wives tales, which you should ignore, and be offered much unwanted advice as to what names the child might be called, but we have time in the months ahead my dearest one to ponder names for a boy or girl. We have been blessed to meet some holy men and women in our travels, so it would be fitting to consider names from The Bible like Adam, David, or Samuel for a son. For a daughter you might like to name her after your mother or Abbess Cecelia who baptised me.

"My Father asks me to have our raven tell Mother that this will be his last sea voyage. With Brother Galen I pray every night for good health and safekeeping in our families, as you, your father and Lady Moya do also."

That night Cormac dreamed of the time when he had first met Grainne, and how he had marvelled at her beauty, re-living using the holy cards had enabled him to rescue her from dying of thirst or drowning after the pirate slavers attacked her ship and captured her father Earl Edwin. When he awoke at dawn, he vowed to not risk his life and that of his companions on this voyage to Brittany, acknowledging his priorities had changed with pending fatherhood.

A cry was heard to come from the lookout in the crow's nest- bad weather approaching, and the wind direction changed abruptly, and sea birds headed for land. Over to larboard they began to see wreckage flying towards them on fierce gales. Approaching rapidly was a large vertically spinning column of water which seemed to suck up the sea and fishes.

All hands were called on deck and Cormac dimly recalled reading about the Greek god Aeolus who had ruled the winds. The anchor was dropped as a precaution and the sails lowered, as steering was becoming an impossibility. The heavy cargo provided some stability, but tall waves threatened to swamp them.

Everyone began to pray and then Brother Galen found himself fingering the phial of holy oil and calling out, "God save us! "He removed the stopper and threw the contents into the raging waters.

Before the eyes of the astonished crew the great spout of water collapsed, the sea became as calm as a mill pond and the winds lessened to a gentle breeze. Shouts of, "It's a miracle, God has answered our prayers!" filled the air and Galen crossed himself and asked the Captain to gather the crew to prayer, who then all knelt down.

Cormac, who had seen what the priest had done, and was somewhat accustomed to the supernatural lifted his hand pointing skywards and said, "Thank God every day of your lives, for we have witnessed Jesus hearing our pleas, and calmed these troubled waters, just like when he was on the Sea of Galilee. "Then Brother Galen led them in a longer prayer of thanksgiving, and two sailors came forward and asked him to hear their Confession.

When the crew had returned to their duties, Captain Huw slapped the priest on the back and said, "Never in my life as sailor and now a captain, have I witnessed such a fortunate occurrence, I must enter it into the ship's log, and I need you to sign the entry with me. You are on the path to sainthood my friend. When I gather with my fellow captains, I will suggest they always carry a priest on their future voyages!"

Cormac then took Brother Galen aside and murmured, "Ever since we met, I have felt the guiding hand of God on the lives of you and myself, and as to the gift of the holy oil, we must make a substantial gift to the gracious donor when we return. Is this a new age of miracles? I am expecting our crew will be more diligent attending Confession in future." Galen smiled and said, "God gave me that oil for a purpose and there is no higher purpose than to save lives. I was wondering if the Greeks or Romans had a word for that great spout of water, it looked like a funnel working in reverse, I suppose it is too silly a word to name it ANTIFUNDIBULUM?"

Looking at the now calm horizon, Cormac joined his father and remarked, "Our armed guards are having a lonely and boring voyage. I feel we should spend time with them; join them at some mealtimes, and you can exchange stories of past battles.

"They also need to be kept fit and alert, so I intend to gather them for exercises, two at a time before each noon hour. Our soldiers seemed to have taken to life aboard ship, so I must get to know them better. Do you have any tall tales of Viking battles that I haven't already heard?"

The four soldiers stood up to attention, recognizing their leaders, and were delighted to share the evening meal with them, particularly since the food, when it arrived was much better than ships rations. Skeggi greeted the men in turn in soldier fashion, each grasping the other's wrists, and said, "Men, you have done well for landlubbers, and kept your station guarding these strong boxes, even when disaster almost struck us, so you can be assured of my good report when we return. Now tell me your names and where you have served?"

COMRADES

The oldest soldier saluted in the old Roman style, forearm across the chest saying, "My name is Barda, and my forebears fought at the Battle of Chester in the year of Our Lord 617. It was a glorious victory over the armies of the Prince of Powys and Bledrus of Cornwall.

"My father and uncle later died from wounds, but bequeathed me this chain mail, and his trusty Gar; its long shaft of ash and iron spear head kept many an enemy at his distance.

"The young lad with the blond hair is my nephew, Chad, he is good with the bow and sling. "He laid a hand on another's shoulder saying, "By my side is my brother of the Shield wall Godwin, he has served with me in the Fryd and is deadly with the Seax in close quarters. Lastly you see before you, Rolf who is half Pict, but chooses not to wear the top knot and blue woad of his tribe. We normally speak for him, as his accent is difficult to understand. He has no tattoos and has never fought naked like his heathen ancestors. We are proud to serve you Lord Skeggi."

Lord Gunnarson called over his son and said proudly, "This is my only son Cormac, and though of similar age to your Chad, he has defeated Pirate slavers and is a clever tactician and designer of Chariots. His New Deva Trading Company charted this vessel and I believe he asked for the four of you personally, claiming a favour from our Earl of Chester who he saved from assassins."

Sir Skeggi's face lit up in a smile and he said, "You have chosen these men well, and we may need this brave band to serve as an honour guard when we meet kings and princes."

The four soldiers cried out, "God save Sir Skeggi and his son, Cormac, we will follow you to the lands of the Middle Sea, if need be."

This pattern of leaders fraternizing with the soldiers began to cause mutters of envy among the sailors and after several days of sailing Captain Huw and Brother Galen reminded them of the morale when favouritism was shown. So, discretely father and son each spent more time with the crew, often during mealtimes and sometimes when sailors kept the night watch, while Cormac climbed into the crow's nest and shared yarns of how important it was to have a lookout with a keen eye warning of other ships, islands, reefs and wreckages.

The simple routines of anchoring at night in a small bay, or a small harbour, and the need to seek fresh drinking water and negotiate local food supplies to vary their diet, meant the time seemed to pass slowly and often tediously.

Captain Huw agreed that they should find a secluded sandy shore where most of the crew could indulge in light-hearted sporting contests. Lord Skeggi and his stepbrother, Mate Rognvald, agreed to captain rival teams that included both crew and soldiers. Manya friendship was made, and not a few sore heads and limbs ensued, the latter tended to by Brother Galen.

Some smaller Welsh kingdoms were avoided as suspicion of Anglo Saxons was rife, but finally they came to the borders of Dyfed and Gwent and Brother Galen asked permission to spend the daylight hours at Porthclais and travel to Glyn Rhosyn as a pilgrimage to the church founded by his hero Dewi . Cormac remembered from his student days at Wroxeter that Dewi was a saintly man who drank only water, even though he died a century ago, his last words had been recorded, "Be joyful and keep your faith."

As the Merlin sailed towards Porthclais, it became evident that it was in decline and all that remained of a harbour was a wall surviving from Roman times, and a few fishing boats at anchor.

Gazing at the cliffs, Sir Skeggi asked, "Where is this holy man's church?"

Galen replied, "Well, first we take the cliff path and then in a grassy hollow, a modest church will be revealed, and a holy well named after Dewi's mother, Non. It is said that Holy Patrick of Ireland foretold Dewi's birth! When we arrive at our destination of Brittany, there he is revered for the many churches he founded in that land."

They left the ship at anchor and began the climb, and Cormac was startled to see flocks of crows and fulmars, disturbed by the pilgrim trio, and Skeggi uttered a mild curse under his breath, as his tunic was spattered with bird lime. Brother Galen grinned, but offered some words of sympathy saying, "I believe the villagers collect the fulmar's eggs, which when cooked have a fishy taste, maybe we can collect some ourselves to supplement our diet?"

Reaching the cliff top, they could now see before them a pleasant grassy hollow in which nestled a modest church with some outbuildings for use by

148

pilgrims. Before entering, they stopped to quench their thirst at Non's well and were greeted in Welsh, 'Diwrnod da, sut wyt ti."

Cormac translated for them, "It means Good Day How are you," and attempted a reply. "Brawd cyfarchion, pererinion ydym niand…" whispered to Galen, "I said, "Greetings brother, we are pilgrims'."

"I am Brother Elfed," he replied in Latin, "the Saxon tongue is not spoken here."

So, during their visit, conversations continued in Latin, with occasional explanation to Skeggi.

Cormac listened carefully as the two priests discussed theology and Elfed spoke proudly of the life of saintly Dewi saying, "You would never have believed from his humble nature, that he was of royal blood and born in the year 500 Anno Domini. He and his followers fed and clothed the needy, cultivated the land and kept beehives. He was made Bishop of Mynyw and was known to oppose Pelagianism because our community believes no-one can earn salvation by their own efforts."

Cormac was fascinated but could see that his father was restless, so they prayed in the church, lit candles for their loved ones, offered a generous donation and accepting four jars of local honey, they made their way back to the ship. Once aboard they consulted the Captain and his mate, Rognvald, as to the course they would now follow, allowing for the currents and the outflow of the estuary of the River Severn.

They would head across to the land of Somerseate, a border country often disputed, but famous for the Roman city of Aquae Sulis, also known as Bath because of the hot springs. The land was still ravaged after the battle between Centwine of Wessex and Welsh King Cadwaladr, but nominally Saxon, so bargaining for fresh food supplies would be difficult and expensive.

Clever Moya

The ship's course had now taken them further south into somewhat hostile lands and so Captain Huw chose only those small inlets where villages were open to trade with those visiting ships that were known to them, and they gladly accepted some amphora's of Portmore Manor wine and cider in exchange for fresh water , fruits and vegetables.

The ancestors of the coastal villages had traded with the Romans many years ago and their modest business in 'silver pigs' of plumbum metal continued.

Before they departed Huw and Rognvald spoke to the crew of a returning fishing boat and were warned of bad weather further south, and so some warm cloaks were purchased. It was then that Cormac recalled his own cloak had been repaired by his mother Moya and a fond memory surfaced of their departure from Ireland over four years ago, and how she had sown silver coins into the hood lining.

Back aboard the *Merlin* he sought out his father and asked, "Did mother provide cloaks for both of us on this voyage?"

Sir Skeggi thought for a moment and then nodded his head saying, "Yes, I packed both of them in a sealskin, but we have not needed them in the recent spell of fine weather, although both cloaks seemed heavier than normal."

So, their personal chests were unlocked, and they found, sewn into the hoods, several gemstones that had come from the pirate hoard. "What a clever resourceful wife I have," said Skeggi. "They will be most useful if we need to bribe someone with influence."

Cormac added, "And maybe afford bringing back gifts for our wives, too."

With full sail the captain hoped to sail around the tip of Dumnonia (some called it West Wales and others Cornwall). Brother Galen remembered reading of this land in a dusty scroll during his training days in Bangor Gwynedd, entitled *'Book of Baglan'* that mentioned legendary King Mark and his castle at Tintagel.

Captain Huw added that on his more recent voyages sailing this coast there was a King named Oswallt ap Cawrdrolli, who despite a Welsh name did not welcome strangers from the north of Wales or Saxons. In Cornwall, there were long memories of Roman armies allegedly trading for Plumbum metal, but covertly looking for healthy slaves. Avoiding a possible hostile encounter, our navigator Huw and Sir Skeggi now hoped to plot a course along the southern coast of Wessex.

FRIEND OR FOE

Next day progress was slow heading against a strong wind from the East when our lookout cried, "Ship on the horizon, closing fast."

Huw, Skeggi and Cormac headed to the ship's prow, while Mate Rognvald climbed up the rigging to better hear more news from the crow's nest.

After what seemed an eternity, our keen-eyed Captain turned to his two companions and exclaimed, "See the unmistakeable carved figurehead of the torso of a woman with an owl perched on her shoulder? It's my Uncle's vessel *The Minerva*. It's not often that our paths cross, but he is a legend in our family, having sailed further east than any captain or navigator I have ever met- he is called Cadfael ap Madoc. His motley crew from many nations mutter among themselves at the chances he takes, and when he is out of earshot, they call him mad dog."

Captain Huw now raised his ship's flag showing a black Merlin on a blue background, then as the two ships drew closer the other ships flag was hoisted- a brown owl on a green background. Huw said proudly, "He only displays that flag when he knows the other ship is friendly, otherwise the flag he raises shows a red dragon."

As the Minerva drew alongside Uncle Cadfael used a leather cone, speaking into it to make his voice carry to his nephew's ship, and a voice boomed out, "Come aboard young Huw, and share a flask of wine, we have much to speak of."

At this the crew of The Merlin, all within earshot began to laugh quietly, for to them their Captain was old. Huw spoke to Mate Rognvald and said, "You have the louder voice, so reply to him- Captain Cadfael, thank you for the invitation, but I would like to bring along and introduce you to two friends who have paid for this voyage and helped navigate us to Brittany on business for the Pope himself."

The crew of both ships set to and threw ropes across and with much strenuous hauling The Merlin and The Minerva were secured safely while sea anchors were lowered and a gangplank from The Minerva allowed the trio to cross slowly over to meet Uncle Cadfael.

He wore a robe of kersey wool and an ornate leather belt with its Owl buckle, wrapped around his enormous waist, and a fancy sword with an ornate handle dangled from a scabbard on his belt. Cadfael had a large beard of dark curly hair but his head was shaven, and weather beaten from the sun of warmer climes.

He wrapped his nephew Huw in a hearty embrace and asked after Huw's wife and son while casting a wary glance at his two visitors. 'What have we here, then? Obviously not from Gwynedd."

Huw answered for them at first saying, "Uncle, I am proud to call these two men my friends, they are Sir Skeggi Gunnarson from the Orkney Isles, famed navigator for the Viking Earl Thorkel and his son, Cormac, born in Portmore, Ireland.

Fruitful Experience

"Oh, a Viking, eh? I have met a few carrot tops on my travels; damn fine warriors and great boat builders. Never pick a fight with 'em, their axes will have an arm or a head off you like Thor's lightning," Madoc replied, half-jokingly.

Skeggi showed his wolf-like grin and said, "I am a settled farmer these days and support my son, Cormac here, in his new trading endeavours. Though I still keep my axe sharp. We are both baptised converts to Christianity and our companion Brother Galen sails with us to heal our ills and pray for safe travel. Our crew thinks he is a saint as his prayers calmed a recent storm with a giant waterspout."

Skeggi asked Madoc, 'What of the lands south of Brittany? I have only sailed to Gotland, Iceland, Ireland, Wales and Mercia?"

The Minerva's Captain asked them to be seated and called for flasks of Frankish wine. They all raised their cups and Cormac proposed a toast. "To our brotherhood of Trading families, may we have calm seas and handsome profits."

Uncle Madoc turned to his nephew, Huw and winked saying, 'Your esteemed captain may have heard some of my tales before and maybe they get a little embellished as I grow older. But first a little food from afar." He called for his cook who bounded off to the ships stores and returned with a platter of round purple objects, in the middle of a pile of small elongated brown things. "I set before you some tasty wonders that come from the lands across the pillars of Hercules. They are sweet fruits and are called figs and dates. Use this knife to cut the round figs in half and you will see the fleshy middle covered in seeds, discard the skins, but eat the rest. The others are dates that contain a stone which you spit out onto this plate."

Cormac cut his fig in half and gazed at the seeds, he could see that they were not like the pips you removed from the apples and pears in his own orchards, but taking a big breath he bit into the fruit and thought it tasted a little like plums but softer and noted that the seeds were soft also, then dropped the fig skin carefully.

Next he swallowed a mouthful of the deep red Frankish wine, and initially thought he preferred Portmore cider, but then a rosy glow suffused his cheeks, and he felt the strong aftertaste of blackberries and cherries and said, "Hmm, this fig and wine would be good to take back to the folk of Chester, have you eaten all the dates, father?"

A contented sigh came from Skeggi and 3 date stones shot out of his mouth onto his plate, and he said, "You can keep those seedy figs, but I will take another cup of that wine."

Then reaching into his leather bag, he took out a sealed flask of Portmore cider saying, "Try this Uncle Cadfael, it will warm the cockles of your heart."

Captain Huw answered, "Two flasks of that cider, Uncle and you will sleep well!"

"Here young Cormac, try some of my dates, watch out for the stones. "So, Cormac carefully bit into the soft flaky flesh of the date and removed the stone, but then with a sly grin on his face, spat the stone out with such force that it hit Madoc on the nose!

Madoc yelped with surprise and said, "I will forgive your youthful prank just once, but next time you try it I will slap your backside."

A Taste of the Future

Madoc spoke softly to Huw, "Before you taste more new delights I need to go aft and talk to you alone."

Then he spoke to his visitors saying, "My cook will bring you 2 more fruits to taste and for these you first need to cut them in half and squeeze the juices into a small cup. Meanwhile I have a family matter to discuss with my nephew, Huw. Then, if we have time, I would like to hear more of your own adventures."

Galen, Skeggi and Cormac were left to drink more wine, but Cormac asked the cook for fresh water, to cleanse his mouth, and the other two agreed.

Huw walked aft until they were both out of earshot and asked, "Is there anything troubling you Uncle, our family see you so rarely?"

Looking sad, Cadfel said, "My dear wife died while I was away on my last voyage and as you know, we have no children, so my usual home coming has lost its joy and purpose. I do not wish to re-marry and my health has not been good since she died. I wish to end my days in Saint Malo, where many speak a version of our native tongue. The sunny days will give my old bones some comfort, as does the local wine. To that end I have had a Notary prepare my Will, and I leave this ship to you, when I die."

Huw was stunned into silence for some moments, then uncharacteristically he gave his uncle and benefactor a hug, wiped away some tears and said gruffly, "You have always seemed so young, vigorous and full of life and mischief. Your success was why I chose to be a sailor and become a captain. You have my heartfelt thanks Uncle, but I hope to be visiting you in Brittany for many voyages to come."

Uncle Cadfael clapped him heartily on the back and remarked, "That's settled then, my notary lives in Bangor, Gwynedd."

Returning to the visitors, no word of this private matter was spoken, and they sat back at the small table and Madoc smiled where a bowl of two brightly coloured round fruits were set, along with small cups. Some fruits were round and the colour of a bright sun, the others seemed to be the colour of expensive saffron.

When Cormac cut the saffron one in half, he saw that the skin was much thicker than his own orchard fruits, and squeezed some juice into his cup, then took a small sip. "What a sweet delicate taste but with some acidity. Is it not ripe?"

Captain Cadfel answered, "All these fruits come from the southern shores of the Kingdom of the Visigoths but are also found around the coast of the lands of the Middle sea. I traded for them in the Frankish port of Marseille, but they came from Visigoth Cartagena. I was warned that these bright juicy fruits do not travel well and may go mouldy before they arrive in Mercia."

Skeggi had already cut and tasted the sunny one and spat out the juice with an oath. "This tastes really sour," he said.

Galen spoke, "Some old Latin scrolls mention this fruit, naming it Citron. They drank it sweetened with honey."

GOSSIP OF BABIES

Back in Portmore Manor by the river Dee, near Chester, the two wives of the Gunnarson family regularly meet for a midday meal that always included Grainne's father, Earl Edwin, who loves to sit and play with Moya's daughter, Julia. The ladies' conversation is always about any news from the voyage of the Merlin that is sailing to Brittany with their husbands, Skeggi and Cormac.

They have occasional visits from Hilda, the wife of Brocmale, the Earl of Chester and her unmarried daughters, who were happy to gossip over sweet cakes and a small cup of Portmore wine. Hilda's younger daughters, Rose and Lily shamelessly flirted with Portmore's young male servants. Ron, Vern, and Peter would always hang around when they saw them arrive by boat; smiling and offering to carry any packages they might bring. Lily would ask indelicate whispered questions to Grainne about how she got with child. As for the mother to be, Grainne had her own unspoken concerns knowing that her own mother had died giving birth to her.

In private, her mother-in law Moya had asked, "When might my first grandchild be expected to be born."

She replied vaguely, "It might be around Pentecost or White Sunday if I counted correctly from when my courses stopped."

Already Grainne needed a maid to help her with bouts of sickness in the mornings, but Moya had reassured her that this circumstance was quite normal. When the visitors had left, she asked Lady Moya, "Please come with me to my bedroom and rest a while, for my back aches somewhat from the child growing in my womb."

When they were alone, she prayed silently, and then aloud, "Odin's raven, come to me that I might send a message to my husband, Cormac."

Their concerns at the delay began to puzzle them, but then they heard the familiar croak 'hrokar, hrokar'. Then in her mind she heard the rebuke, "I have my own brood to feed, and Yggdrasil has no fruit or worms for my little chicks."

A contrite Grainne replied, "Forgive me, for soon I will have my own baby to feed." She asked the raven politely, "Please wing your way to the ship, the *Merlin*, heading for Brittany and say, "Dearest

162

husband my bed is so lonely without you. Your own mother misses Skeggi. What news do you have of your progress and when will you return home? I think our child will be born at Pentecost."

"Your hopeless trio of protégés, Vern, Peter and Ron have big appetites and are showing an interest in maidens. Harvests have been good this year. Greet your father, Brother Galen and Captain Huw and give them my news."

Even now, both ladies marvelled that Odin's raven did not enter through a window or door, but just appeared, and now with Grainne's message complete, the raven disappeared.

Farewells

With Huw's thoughts of inheriting The Minerva still whirling around in his head, he bid them raise a final glass of thanks for his Uncle Cadfael's hospitality and wished his benefactor a safe voyage home before they crossed over back to his own ship.

Galen asked for silence and offered a prayer for the future safety of both ships. Captain Madoc replied quietly, "That Skeggi and his lad, Cormac, were fine company and I could not resist seeing their faces when I offered the Citron fruit juice for tasting. I envy you your Viking navigator, even though this may be my last voyage. Young Cormac's tales of pirate's lairs and constructing a roman-style chariot were fascinating; he will be a lad with a great future, someday. Having a priest and healer sailing with you is a blessing, indeed."

Uncle Madoc and Huw embraced each other and slapped each other's shoulders, while Skeggi and his son shook the hand of their host. Cormac said, "It's been an honour to meet you Captain, those new fruits you shared with us are worth more consideration as trade goods, if only someone can find a way to keep them fresh for Chester market."

Uncle Cadfael smiled and said, "Good luck with that, but here is the cook who wishes to hand over the box of fruits which my crew do not care for, and would otherwise, throw them away. My nephew told me that you have a beautiful wife that awaits your return. When you are aboard The Merlin, look for an extra gift from the land of the Visigoths for her, wrapped up and underneath the fruits."

A little puzzled, Cormac accepted the box of fruits with embarrassed and effusive thanks, and so the trio crossed over back to their ship, and the ropes were unhitched, freeing each vessel to continue their journey.

A wild guilty thought came into Cormac's mind. Should he have abandoned this voyage and asked for passage home with Cadfael to be with his wife and unborn child? But that would mean that he had failed his own creation: THE NEW DEVA TRADING COMPANY and its shareholders. He would be found unworthy of the trust of Abbott Peter to safely deliver the strong boxes to Brittany and dreams of a Trading Empire would be shattered.

They were greeted by Mate Rognvald who had been anxious for their safety aboard a strange vessel and a relieved smile beamed from his face as he said, "Well my captain, it's good to have you back. The crew have been a little restless, so we have been enjoying some friendly sporting contests, including wrestling matches; with solders Barda and Chad declared the winners."

Skeggi and Huw thanked the mate for his skill in keeping the crew fit and active, for boredom was known to foster quarrels. While the crew gathered around, the captain informed them, "We will set sail when they have rested from their friendly combat, and all would be offered some rare new fruits from lands beyond the Pillars of Hercules; a gift from Captain Madoc. They would also be offered a small cup of wine from the land of the Franks."

Carrying the gift box of fruits, Cormac headed to the galley to advise the cook and greet him. He unpacked the box and explained, pointing, "These are figs with edible seeds, those are sweet dates with stones, and the larger round brightly coloured fruits need to be cut in half. These, when cut would need to be on separate larger platters. I will join you a little later to explain to the crew."

Carrying the wrapped item that had been beneath the fruits, he joined his father and Galen and showed them saying, "This is a mysterious gift from Captain .Cadfael" Then he removed the wrapping to reveal a beautiful, coloured glass brooch mounted in bronze depicting an eagle on a pin. Galen gasped in awe, "This is for pinning a cloak; it's called an Eagle Fibula, rare and precious, made by Visigoth craftsmen."

WITHIN SPITTING DISTANCE

Cormac decided to sew the precious Eagle Fibula brooch into the hood of his cloak for safety. Meanwhile his father, Captain Huw and Brother Galen had an amusing time introducing Rognvald, the cook and crew to the delights of four new fruits. Skeggi howled with glee when he saw his stepbrother's face when he was first to taste and grimaced spluttering, "This juice is more sour than crab apples."

More merriment followed when Galen obliged by showing how to not swallow the date stones. Thus, began a contest between the soldiers and the sailors on who could spit a date stone into a metal bowl from a distance of two arms-length. The guard Rolf was the winner! All agreed the sour citron fruit juice and pulp was much improved by a spoonful of honey and their least favourite was the fig, not being used to eating the tiny seeds.

As they sailed past the island of Vectis, the open sea was their next heading and Cormac readily took instruction from the Captain and his father in the use of Viking navigation tools and recognizing the stars in the night sky when at anchor. Other times, honing his leadership skills, he spent time with the soldiers and crew who were on watch duties.

Unable to sleep, he put on the tarn helm to wander around the ship invisible and be alone with his thoughts of home. The now familiar wing beat, and hoarse cry of Odin's raven disturbed his reverie. The bird unerringly settled on his arm that was entwined in the rigging. His mind was flooded with the message from his beloved Grainne and he even saw through the bird's beady eyes, the faces of his mother and wife, whose belly was now gently rounded.

Her news that their baby might be born at Pentecost. It was then his own loneliness almost overcame him, as he knew it was unlikely that he would sail home in time for the birth. Nevertheless, he felt blessed that Grainne was safe and well, and in their home surrounded by family and friends.

He said to Odin's raven, "Return to Portmore Manor and tell my wife and mother that I have met Captain Huw's Uncle Cadfael and we dined on his ship The Minerva and tasted some new fruits from far off lands. I wish I could devise a way to bring some home for you, but except for the dates (which I'm told grow in clusters on palm trees) the citron fruits and the figs may not survive the return voyage.

"Please eat well for the sake of our baby, and do not undertake any strenuous tasks-leave that to the servants. You know this trading voyage is important for our future and the investors are relying on me, otherwise I did think about leaving the tasks to my father and sailing home with the Minerva. We are leaving the shores of Wessex and crossing the sea to Brittany, where our destiny awaits."

THE END

Follow the further adventures of Trader Cormac in Book 3.

Author Mike Brain

was born in Birmingham, England. He has lived in North Wales for over 40 years. He graduated from Aston University studying Polymer Chemistry & Plastics Technology.

Most of Mike's working life was spent in R & D laboratories, specializing in Adhesives including a 2-year secondment to Dunlop Canada, Toronto.

He is a sometime member of British Science Fiction Association, enjoying Novocon conventions and meeting authors.

Mike is currently a member of the Dorothy Dunnett Society. He enjoys Historical fiction and fantasy.

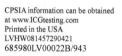